DATE DUE

Demco, Inc. 38-293

*Bring
Me
Your
Saddest
Arizona*

The

John

Simmons

Short

Fiction

Award

University of

Iowa Press

Iowa City

Ryan
Harty

Bring
Me
Your
Saddest
Arizona

University of Iowa Press, Iowa City 52242

Printed in the United States of America

http://www.uiowa.edu/uiowapress

The publication of this book was generously supported by the
University of Iowa Foundation and the National Endowment
for the Arts.

Printed on acid-free paper

Library of Congress Cataloging-in-Publication Data

Harty, Ryan, 1965–

Bring me your saddest Arizona / by Ryan Harty.

p. cm.—(The John Simmons short fiction award)

Contents: What can I tell you about my brother?—
Ongchoma—Between Tubac and Tumacacori—Crossroads—
Sarah at the palace—Why the sky turns red when the sun goes
down—Don't call it Christmas—September.

ISBN 0-87745-869-3 (pbk.)

1. Southwestern States—Social life and customs—Fiction.

I. Title.   II. Series.

PS3608.A7878B75 2003

813'.6—dc21   2003042643

03   04   05   06   07   P   5   4   3   2   1

For Julie

and for my family

Contents

ACKNOWLEDGMENTS

Stories in this collection have appeared in the
following publications: "What Can I Tell
You about My Brother?" in *Playboy*; "Ongchoma" in the *Missouri Review*; "Why the
Sky Turns Red When the Sun Goes Down"
in *Tin House*, *The Best American Short Stories 2003*, and *The 2003 Pushcart Prize An-
thology*; and "Don't Call It Christmas" in the
Missouri Review.

I owe thanks to many people: to my teachers,
especially Jim Krusoe, John L'Heureux and
Tobias Wolff, for indispensable guidance and
encouragement; to my friends and readers,
especially Peter Rudy, Aaron Cohen, and
Tom Barbash, for insight and support; to my
wonderful agent, Kim Witherspoon, and to
the remarkable Alexis Hurley at Witherspoon Associates; to Evelyn Somers and Bob
Burchfield, for their uncanny editorial skills;
to everyone at the Iowa Press for the hard
work they put into publishing this book; to
the Iowa Writers' Workshop and the Stegner
Fellowship at Stanford University, for provid-
ing the time it took to write these stories;
and most of all to my amazing wife, Julie
Orringer, for being everything to me.

*Bring
Me
Your
Saddest
Arizona*

What Can
I Tell You
about My
Brother?

On his first night home from marine boot camp,
my brother killed Rob Dawson's German shepherd with a Phillips
screwdriver. Rob was the captain of my football team at Arcadia
High School. He was an all-league quarterback and a popular guy,
and since the end of the summer he'd been seeing a girl named
Jessica Lynn Armstrong, who'd gone out with my brother before

he joined the marines. She and Victor had been together for a year and a half, and they'd been serious enough to talk about getting married after he finished boot camp. But during his tenth week of training, she called to say she was seeing Rob, and it must have made my brother crazy. He killed the dog in the backyard of the Dawsons' house, a three-story Spanish villa overlooking the whole sleeping valley. He left the body floating on the lighted blue pool, disappeared over a row of yuccas, and didn't come home until the next afternoon.

Late that night, as I lay in bed, I heard the chirp of tires through my open window. A car door slammed, and then Rob Dawson was screaming at my dad through the screen door, banging his hand against the jamb. My dad's voice was thick with sleep or drink. I lay in my dark room, ten feet away, listening through the open window.

"You let me talk to Victor!" Rob yelled, his voice high pitched and loud. His shoes squeaked on the cement porch floor.

"Victor's not home," my dad said. "What the hell is this about?"

"He fucking killed my dog!" Rob said, and threw a fist at the screen. I thought he'd try to bust into the house.

"Settle down," my dad said. "You've made a mistake. Victor wouldn't do anything like that."

"It was him," Rob said. "I know he's back in town."

I pressed my cheek against the window. In the glow of the porch lamp, Rob's face was pale and drawn. I didn't know him well. Though we played on the same team, I was two years younger and had spoken to him only once or twice.

"Just tell me where he is," he said.

"He's gone," my dad said. "He's not here."

"I swear I'll kill the son of a bitch."

My dad said something I couldn't make out, and then Rob stopped shouting and stared into the house, his mouth falling open. It took me a few seconds to realize my dad was crying.

"Oh, Victor," he cried—not near the door, but somewhere inside the house now, close to my room. "What the hell has he *done?*"

Rob ran to the Jeep, which was still idling at the curb. He got in and laid a strip of rubber down the blacktop.

I listened to my father sobbing, a muted noise almost like laughter. The screen door opened, and he stepped onto the lawn, dressed in a pale blue robe and corduroy slippers. He stared at the end of the street for a while before going back inside, and then I heard him moving from room to room, talking to himself in a low, troubled voice. There was a time when he would have waited for Victor to come home and then beat the hell out of him. But he was old now; his heart was bad. There wasn't much he could do.

The next day after practice I showered and changed, then went back to the field to look for a lens that had come out of my glasses during drills. As I crawled on hands and knees around the blocking sleds, I was thinking about my dad, who could get ugly when he had to buy new glasses all the time. It was a cloudy day, with a breeze coming over a row of ironwood trees. I kept picturing Victor in the dim light on Camelback Mountain, his hair shaved off for the marines.

I was still searching for the lens when Rob Dawson came out of the locker room, shirtless, a duffel bag slung over his shoulder. I'd seen him in practice that afternoon and had been afraid of what he might say to me, but he'd never met my gaze. Now he came down the asphalt strip that led to the practice field, right toward me.

"What are you doing?" he called. My voice cracked as I explained.

He started to search for the lens with me, not on all fours but bent over just slightly, his wet hair combed back in rows.

"It's no big deal," I said, because I just wanted him to leave me alone.

He bent down and parted the grass with his fingers. The lens winked in the sun as he held it up.

"Oh man," I said, "I didn't think I'd find it."

"You didn't," he said, and tossed it to me, a faint smirk on his face. He sat down on the grass beside me.

It would have been awkward to leave at that point, though that's what I wanted to do. All day people who had heard about my brother had stared at me as if I'd killed Rob's dog myself.

Rob plucked grass with his fingers, seeming to find interest in something behind me. Then he narrowed his eyes and said, "So, what can you tell me about your brother?"

"What do you mean?" I asked.

"I've been asking people about him," he said. "So far I've only heard he's an asshole. I want to know if there's anything good about him. Most of the time, you know, there's some good thing about everyone."

I turned the lens in my fingers, thinking. There *were* good things about Victor, I knew, but there were plenty of bad things. He'd beaten me up and embarrassed me, had treated me in ways that would have made me hate him if he were anyone else. But he had protected me, too. He was my brother, and what I felt was complicated. I had no idea how to explain it to someone whose dog he'd killed.

"He's kind of an asshole," I said finally, just wanting to leave.

Rob nodded. He didn't seem surprised. He stood and brushed dead grass from his Levi's and said, "Come on. I'll give you a ride home."

"All right," I said. But as soon as I said it I wished I hadn't.

——— ———

When I was twelve and my brother was fifteen, I knocked over the ironing board and burned a hole in the kitchen linoleum. My dad completely lost his head. He held me down and touched the iron to the back of my neck, blistering the skin. I ran out into the empty street, screaming. The curtains parted in the houses all around me. I touched my neck where my skin still felt like it was burning. After a moment my brother came out the front door, his arms full of bottles, a look of determination on his face.

"Okay, now," he said as he crossed the lawn. "Here we go, Tommy."

One of the bottles broke as he set them on the sidewalk, and he said, "That's my point. Right there's my fucking point." He grinned at me, his eyes small and wild. Then he picked up a bottle, threw it end over end at the house, and it shattered against a brick column that held up the carport.

He handed me one. "Do it," he said, his long hair hanging in his face.

I threw the bottle. Victor let out a high-pitched whoop as it exploded in the driveway. In a minute, my dad appeared in the front doorway, wearing navy blue coveralls and work boots. He stared at me like he was waiting for me to throw another bottle, like he was daring me to, but I couldn't, not while he was there. I waited until he'd gone inside, and then I threw a few more. Victor kept handing them to me. I started laughing as I threw them and couldn't stop, though I was crying still. Wiping a forearm across his face, Victor said, "Yeah! Do it, Tommy! Do it!"

This might have been the kind of thing Rob wanted to hear— a good thing about my brother. But I didn't think he'd understand it, coming from where he did, and I didn't think it was any of his business.

The inside of Rob's Jeep smelled of cologne and leather, and the dash looked as if it had never been spilled on. I hoped he'd ask for directions, so we could both pretend he hadn't been to my house the night before. But he drove south down Yavapai, toward the low houses of my neighborhood. Rob lived exactly the other way. If you looked you could see his house and a few dozen others set in among the saguaros on Camelback Mountain.

After Victor called to tell me about Rob and Jessica, I started seeing them everywhere together—eating lunch by the Papago Fountain, walking together through the quad. At first they were usually alone, but little by little she started hanging out with Sophia Elkin and Bradley Scott, Rob's other friends. It was strange to see her with that crowd, she was so unlike them—a kind of tough girl who wore cuffed jeans and would let you know if she was pissed at you. She was pretty, though, which was what you had to be, I guess, and she could be fun to be around when she was in a good mood. People seemed to respect her.

Rob glanced at me. "I watched you in practice today," he said. "You run a quick pattern. You should get some playing time."

"I don't think so," I said. I was one of the fastest players on the team but was only a sophomore, and small, a second-string flanker brought up from JV.

We came to a red light, and Rob looked at the empty lots where Mexicans sold painted pottery. "How'd you like to get in the game against the Pimas on Friday night?"

"How?" I asked.

"Don't worry about that." The light changed, and he accelerated through the intersection.

"I don't know," I said. The game against the Pimas would be our biggest of the season, with both teams coming in undefeated. We'd play under the bright lights at the reservation stadium, which was always crowded with Indians from the Pima-Maricopa community. I had a hard time concentrating on any of that, though, with the other things on my mind: Victor and my dad and Rob's dog, which was what I'd thought Rob would want to talk to me about.

"I guess I'd like it," I said.

"I bet."

We were coming into the rows of pastel-painted houses, passing the street where Jessica lived with her stepdad, who worked on the line with my dad at Motorola. Rob looked down the street as we passed. A police car sat in front of one of the houses. I thought it might be there for Jess's brother, Matt, who'd been in trouble for selling pot.

"Did you wonder why I didn't call the cops?" he asked.

"I figured you had."

"That's not how I do things," he said, looking evenly out at the road ahead. But then his face fell, and he had to tighten his grip on the steering wheel.

"I'm sorry it happened," I said.

"Hey, it's not your fault."

I couldn't help thinking it *was* my fault, though—that I had to share the blame in some way. We were turning onto my own street now, which seemed more rundown than usual, with a lot of cars up on blocks and toddlers playing on the sidewalks in their underwear. I saw Victor lying on a towel in our front yard, bare chested, wearing cutoffs. Rob saw him, too, and pulled to the curb. He let his eyes fall to the dash.

"If you think I know what to do right now, you're wrong," he said, then smiled suddenly, glancing at me. "I've got no fucking idea."

"Maybe you don't have to do anything," I said.

But he was already opening the door, stepping outside. He went around the front of the Jeep, where he paused, watching my brother, who still hadn't seen us. "All right," Rob said, quietly, almost to himself, then banged his palm once on the metal hood and bolted into the yard. I got out of the car and stood there, my hand still on the handle.

Victor hadn't quite gotten to his feet when Rob hit him the first time. He ducked his head and raised his hands to protect his face, but Rob got in a few sharp jabs to the back of his neck. I heard a dull thud each time he connected. Victor tried to turn, but Rob was staying in front of him, rotating his chest, swinging with both hands. Even hunched over, my brother was as tall as Rob. I knew he'd been in a lot of fights before and had lost very few of them. But he wasn't even trying now. He just slumped around in his bare feet, his head jerking each time Rob connected.

"Fight me!" Rob said, trying to lift my brother up by the shoulders. "Fight me, you son of a bitch!"

Victor raised his head. His face was slack and drained of emotion. "Fuck it," he said. "Hit me, man. You want to hit me, hit me."

Rob backed off. "You're an asshole," he said, breathing hard. "Everyone's told me that, even your brother."

I turned away when Victor looked at me. I wasn't used to seeing him with his hair shaved off, and he looked ridiculous—his head too small, his nose too long for his face. A line of blood ran down from his eyebrow. And then he started coughing and had to buckle over with his fist at his mouth.

"You're pathetic," Rob said, leaning forward as if to be sure Victor heard him. "What do you have to say for yourself?"

"Nothing," my brother said.

"Is something just the matter with you?"

"Must be."

Rob made a small, disgusted noise in his throat. He gave me a quick look, then turned and walked across the lawn to his Jeep, which was still idling at the curb. I watched the Jeep speed to the end of the street and disappear around the corner.

"Jesus, Tommy," Victor said. "I really needed that."

"I didn't think you'd be here."

"You brought him home," he said. "You brought him right to our *house*." He blew out a laugh and let himself fall onto the towel, then coughed a few times into his fist.

I sat down beside him, looking at the horizon, which was dark blue and getting darker.

"Check out this tan, man," Victor said, holding his arms out, trying to be funny—trying, I suppose, to make me forget why Rob had beaten him up in the first place. His face, neck, and arms were brown, while the rest of him was bone-white. The line of blood was drying on his collarbone. "It's embarrassing," he said.

I watched a jet plane pull a line of white over the peaks of the Phoenix Mountains.

"Tiny O'Smallessey here," Victor said.

It was a joke from around the time when our mom died. To be Tiny O'Smallessey was to be as low as you could be. When we were kids, the two of us had done skits in which we were Tiny and Teeny, the O'Smallessey Brothers. Victor looked at me, and the smile fell from his face.

"You probably think I'm crazy," he said.

"I think you're stupid."

"Fair enough. I'll catch shit for it, though. More shit. Watch."

"He didn't call the cops," I told him.

"How do you know that?"

"He just told me."

He nodded again but didn't seem relieved. "He should have called them. I would have called them if it was my dog." Then he narrowed his eyes and said, "You think I don't feel bad about it?"

"I don't know," I said. "I hope you do."

"Would you believe it was like something I couldn't control?"

"I don't know what I'd believe."

"That's the way I'd describe it," he said, a pained look on his face. "Like something I couldn't control. Though it seems like bullshit now, even to me."

It seemed it to me, but I didn't say so.

In the west, the clouds had come together like a dark gray mountain. The air was wet and getting cooler. My brother told me what had happened—that he had gone to Rob's house with a screwdriver and a bucket of sand, intending to sabotage the Dawsons' pool pump. But when he got there, the idea seemed suddenly pointless: the houses on the hill were so big and the people in them had so much money that they could just have the pump fixed and be swimming the next day, if they wanted. You'd have to do something serious to get to them, he thought. In boot camp he'd heard stories about the Viet Cong leaving dead South Vietnamese babies outside U.S. camps, trying to break the GIs down mentally.

"I don't know," he said. "I saw the dog, you know? He was barking, making a lot of noise. Something clicked in me. At some point I realized what I was doing, but by then he was already dead. I was just crazy, Tommy. I swear I was crazy the whole time. When I put him in the pool I felt almost like myself, but I wasn't quite myself still." He looked up. "Do you have any idea what I'm talking about?"

"I wish I did," I said. "But then again I'm glad I don't."

"Yeah, right," he said. "Bingo."

———

At practice on Thursday Coach Harding worked me in with the starting offense in scrimmage, but I was nervous and bobbled passes. Everyone had a reason to be mad at me. If it wasn't because I was a sophomore starting over a senior, it was because of what my brother had done. The defense knew which plays we would run, and were supposed to compensate by not going full-out, but on four straight slants I got my clock cleaned. After knocking the wind out of me one time, Tim Zucher pointed at Rob and said, "That was for you, buddy."

Rob pretended he hadn't heard him.

In the locker room he avoided me, but he caught up to me in the parking lot and said, "Don't worry about what happened today. You'll be fine tomorrow night."

"I got fucking killed," I said.

"Don't worry about that," he said. "You're a tough kid. You can handle it."

I touched a hand to a rib that felt like it might be broken. "Fuck off, man," I said.

Victor wasn't around when I got home that night, and my dad was in his bedroom, watching a football game. I sat on the couch in the living room and went over my playbook. My dad and I hardly ever talked anymore, which was how both of us sort of wanted things. We'd fallen into a kind of quiet routine after his heart attack.

As I studied, I thought about Victor running around somewhere with his stupid haircut, doing God knows what. It made it hard to concentrate. I had a lot of studying to do, because the plays we ran on varsity were different than the ones we'd run on JV. After a while, a pizza man came to the front door, and my dad came out and paid him, then took the pizza into his bedroom. Twenty minutes later, he came back and dropped half the pizza on the coffee table.

"Where's Victor?" I asked.

"How the hell do I know? Hasn't he gone back already?"

"Not till tomorrow."

He pinched his eyebrows together. "He in some kind of trouble? A kid came by the other night, looked like he meant to give Victor a hard time."

"I don't know anything about it," I said.

"This kid was a goddamn pain in the ass," he said, and gave a hard laugh. "I almost had to bust him a new one."

I got up and went to the kitchen for some paper towels.

"Hey, I'm watching the Cards," he said, jerking a thumb behind him. "If you're interested. They're beating the shit out of the Rams."

"I've got to study my plays," I said. "I think I'm going to get into the game on Friday."

"Is that right?" He was suddenly nervous, rubbing his palms down the sides of his robe. It had been a while since I'd mentioned anything personal, and I don't think he knew how to handle it. Finally, he just said, "That's great, kid," and went back toward the bedroom. I heard the sound of the football game as he opened the door.

* * *

Victor came home the next afternoon when I was there to pick up my playbook. His clothes were a mess, and he was tired looking and on edge. I saw the black cut over his eyebrow where Rob had hit him.

"Where have you been?" I asked.

"Out," he said, hurrying past me. "But I've got to get to the bus station now."

My dad was asleep in his bedroom. Victor changed into his uniform, then found my dad's car keys, and the two of us walked out to the truck.

It was a crisp day, the sun cool and white. We took 68th to Mc-Dowell, keeping on the surface streets because my dad's truck wasn't registered.

"So where did you go last night, anyway?" I asked.

Victor laughed, more relaxed now that we were on our way. "Nowhere," he said. "Well, actually, right up this road. I hitch-hiked. I got a ride halfway to the bus station, then changed my mind."

"How did you get back?"

"Walked," he said, and laughed again. "Last night I slept in Papago Park. I was using my survival training. Hey, do you remember when we went out and looked for that boy who was lost?"

Just before he left for the marines, Victor, Jessica, and I had joined a search party to find a Cub Scout who'd wandered away from his pack in the desert to the north. We spent a couple of days searching around Cave Creek, though we found nothing but pieces of bleached ironwood that looked like bones. Eventually, after Victor left, the boy's body turned up in a dry riverbed west of Carefree.

"Did you ever hear what happened to that kid?" Victor asked.

"He was all right," I lied. "They found him just after you left."

"Okay, good. I never knew."

We went past the twin buttes and the National Guard base. Up ahead was something on the side of the road, a pyramid shape. Victor leaned forward, squinting at it.

I couldn't make it out until we got closer, and then I saw what it was: a formation of rocks set back in a field, a perfectly symmetrical pyramid that stood as tall as a man.

"Look at that," Victor said, and seemed suddenly excited. "Somebody built that, you know? That's a job I think I could handle."

"It's not a real job," I said. "No one gets paid for it."

"Still, though. Just doing it for the hell of it."

I watched the pyramid get smaller in the rearview mirror. "You haven't told me much about the marines."

Victor stared at a stretch of paloverdes that ran along the road. "There are some tough motherfuckers in there," he said, shaking his head. "Real salty dudes."

"You don't like it at all?"

"You just deal with it," he said, and shrugged. "I don't like it, though, no. I fucking hate it." He leaned back against the seat, biting his bottom lip. "They've got this thing that messes with your head, where they punish everyone in the unit every time one guy fucks up. So you know me, right? I've always been a fuckup. And so I'll just pull some bullshit thing—mouthing off or slacking or just doing something wrong by accident—and suddenly everyone's doing squat-jumps on my behalf or running the perimeter. It makes it hard to have friends. People don't like me there. I'm not a good soldier, though I wish I was. I'd like to be."

We went under the interstate, then passed a few taquerias and hubcap shacks. I felt like I should say something reassuring, but nothing came to mind. We didn't speak until we'd pulled up beside the bus station.

"Well," I said, "good luck, I guess. I'll see you at Christmas, right?"

He nodded, opening the truck door. Then he closed it again and said, "Hey, so how's Dad been lately?"

"All right, I guess."

He narrowed his eyes at me, almost as if he were angry. "How's he *been*, though, I mean. With you."

"All right," I said. "No big problems."

"Okay, good," he said, and opened the door again. He set his duffel bag on the sidewalk, got out and closed the door, then leaned in the window, grinning. "I used to always ask you to show me your muscle, remember that? To flex? And now it's actually pretty big." He reached in and squeezed my bicep. "I never thought it would be, for some reason."

"It's not that big," I said.

"It's not bad," he said. "Man, I wish I could watch your game tonight."

"Me too. I think I'm going to get some playing time."

But he was distracted, staring at the metal dash and the overflowing ashtrays, at the crushed beer cans on the floor. He turned and looked at the station, where an old man sat eating an apple on a bench beside the door. I could only see the side of Victor's face, but he looked worried. He'd come back to a place where his girlfriend was no longer his girlfriend, then had killed a dog and gotten beaten up for it, and now, it seemed, he didn't want to leave. But he turned and slung the duffel bag over his shoulder. As he disappeared through the station doors, his head was so unfamiliar with the new haircut that he almost could have been someone I'd never met.

At the postgame party at Sophia Elkin's I drank beer and looked at all the paintings on the walls. There were a few oils that looked like the stages of a dust storm, going from beige to brown, and several watercolors of desert landscapes. Sophia's house was big and open, with red leather furniture and hardwood floors. She lived on Camelback Mountain, a few houses down from Rob.

We had beaten the Pimas by fourteen points, and I'd had a big game, six receptions and a short TD sweep around the left side. It was a bigger deal because I'd been up against Sammy Yava, an all-league cornerback who'd signed a letter of intent with ASU. He was a wiry kid, with quick eyes and silver cuffs around his front teeth. I talked to him after the game. He told me he had a wife and kid already, which blew my mind. He was only two years older than I was.

Mostly there were juniors and seniors at the party, Camelback and Paradise Valley people, all of whom I recognized but none of whom I knew well. Rob Dawson stumbled over with his arm around Jess, who wore a black dress I hadn't seen. Her hair was cut shorter in the back, with the bangs still long. She seemed nervous until I smiled at her, and then she smiled back and said, "Hey, Tommy. You were great tonight."

"Thanks," I said.

Rob leaned in and said, "I was right about you, Pendcrest. How does it feel to be a superstar?" He was drunk and had asked me that already on the car ride over.

"Not bad," I said.

"Stick with me," he said. "You'll go places." Then he put an arm around Jess, and she let him lead her away, though she glanced back and rolled her eyes at me.

"Where's Tommy Pendcrest?" Tim Zucher was saying behind me, sitting at a table with a group of big linemen. "Where's Pendcrest?" He grinned and looked around as if he couldn't find me. He had a big bottle of Jaegermeister and a shot glass. He poured me a shot.

"All right, you tough little shit," he said, handing it over.

I had to close my eyes after I'd drunk it, which made everyone crack up.

I wandered away, feeling my face go warm. There was a line for the bathroom by the kitchen, so I found another one on the second floor, a bathroom as big as my bedroom at home, with a sunken tub and a shower wide enough for two people at a time. The window by the toilet looked out on the backyard. As I peed I stared at the lighted patio, where people milled around, the wavy lines of the pool lighting their faces. I couldn't help imagining a dead dog in the water.

Rob and Jess and a few others were talking about a trip they were going to take to Mexico over Christmas break. Rob had mentioned it on the car ride over. Carl Mathers came out of the house with a bottle of wine and said, "So, Rob, that fucker ever go back to the army?"

"Just today," Rob said.

"Man," Carl said, "I'd have fucked the son of a bitch up big time if it was me. Anybody messes with my dog."

"I fucked him up," Rob said, looking into his plastic cup of beer.

"I can't waste my time with that shit, though, you know? The guy's a fucking psychopath."

"No shit," Carl said. "Hey, no offense, Jess."

Everyone laughed at that. Jess gave Carl a look as if she might lay into him, but she only flipped him off and walked away. Rob followed her.

I drew back from the window. I had a feeling in my chest like homesickness.

Downstairs, nearly everyone was drinking shots in the kitchen. I saw Rob and Jess in the dining room, talking quietly. I went into the empty living room, stole a brass lighter someone had left on the coffee table, then walked out the front door.

Outside, Sophia's yard sloped up to a kind of rounded peak, and I climbed up and stood on the top, looking down at the town and working the lighter. It was cool out, and I could see every-thing—downtown and the university and Papago Park. A full moon shone through the clouds, lighting the hills around me.

After a while I started down Valle Vista Road toward home. In the house next to Sophia's, a man stared at me from a second-story window, and I stared back until he went away.

Rob Dawson's house was down on the right, all the windows dark, his Jeep parked in the long circular driveway. Around the side of the house someone was peeing on a tree in the shadows, and I knew right away that it was Victor. He tried to duck behind the tree, then saw who I was and stepped into the light. He wore his uniform, which was wrinkled around the crotch and knees.

"I just ended up here," he said. "It's not like I've got a plan or anything."

"Aren't you supposed to be back by now?"

"Well, I'm AWOL," he said with a small smile. "Probably be in deep shit when I go back. I saw you play tonight, though. I went to the game, and you were great." He cocked his head in the di-rection I'd come from. "Were you just at that party?"

I said I was.

"I don't know what I'm supposed to do," he said, seeming wor-ried all of a sudden. "Seems like I should just do something, you know? I keep having this feeling that something's supposed to happen."

"We should go home," I said. "You should go back to the marines."

He blew out a laugh. "I don't exactly want to see Dad right now."

He walked to the curb and sat with his feet in the gutter. All the lights were out at Rob's, a big three-story house with a lot of wrought iron and Spanish tile. "Did you ever used to think she was in love with me?" Victor asked. "Back when we were together still?"

"I suppose I did."

He scraped his boots on the blacktop, pulling his knees to his chest. "Like, I think a lot about when Dad was in the hospital and she'd come with me to visit him every day. I probably thought more about her than I thought about Dad, which sounds terrible, but it's true. It seemed like we would be together for the rest of our lives, you know? It didn't seem crazy to think that."

"It wasn't crazy at the time," I said.

"It's not true, now," he said, "I realize that." He faced the houses on the other side of the street. "I do want to do something, though. I feel like there must be one thing that if I could just think of it, you know?"

"Doing things only gets you in trouble," I said.

"I know you're right," he said.

The dusty smell of the air let me know it would rain soon. A car drove by, sweeping us with its headlights, and then I heard a noise and looked up the hill. Two people were coming down the sidewalk, talking in quiet voices. I realized it could be Rob and Jess, coming back to Rob's. But the light was too dim to see them.

"Let's go," I said.

Victor nodded, scraping the dried paloverde leaves with his boots. He glanced up the street and narrowed his eyes.

"Jesus, that's them, isn't it?" he said.

"I don't know," I said. "Let's just get out of here."

The couple came under a streetlight, and I saw that it was them. Rob was the first to see us, and he stopped. In a sharp voice, he called, "What the fuck's going on, Pendcrest? What are you two doing here?"

"We were just leaving," I said.

"You'd *better* leave."

Victor stood. "Hey, Jess, can I talk to you?" he asked.

Jess glanced down the hill at the valley, her long bangs hanging in her face.

"She doesn't want to," Rob said. "You can see that, can't you?"

"She does, though," Victor said. "Come on, Jess. Don't treat me like Tiny O'Smallessey."

She smiled, looking at him—a surprise to me, because I didn't think she'd know what he was talking about. Her expression was sympathetic and warm, though there might have been some pity in it, too.

Rob gave a hard laugh, shaking his head as if the world had suddenly gone crazy around him. "Jesus, talk to him then," he said, and walked down the hill toward me.

Victor jogged up to Jess. I heard him say something quiet, then laugh and add, "Okay, I'll make it simple." He stood with his back to me and Rob, lowering his voice so we couldn't hear him.

"So what's the story, Pendcrest?" Rob asked me.

"I don't know," I said. "I didn't mean for any of this to happen."

"You better get your priorities straight," he said in a dark tone.

It didn't matter what he said, though. He'd helped me get some playing time and now he seemed to think I'd betrayed him, which was ridiculous. He should have known that if it came to a choice between my brother and someone else, I'd always choose Victor. I walked to the edge of the road, where I could see the hazy, glittering skyline of Phoenix.

Above me Jess said, "No, Victor," and I glanced up there. She was smiling, staring down at something my brother held in front of him. The two of them laughed.

"This is bullshit," Rob said, throwing his cup of beer on the lawn. "Jess, I'm going inside." He started toward the door.

Then Victor finished talking and came down the sidewalk, and Jess walked across the grass to catch up with Rob. She waved good night to me, and I waved back. Rob opened the front door, and she followed him inside.

"So what happened?" I asked after the door had closed.

"Well, it went well," Victor said, nodding, starting down Valle Vista. "It went pretty good, I think."

"What did you say?"

"Well, I told her I was sorry about that dog," he said with a grim look. "Jesus, that wasn't easy. For a minute I thought she'd cry, but she didn't. She knows me pretty well. She said I must have just been crazy at the time, which is exactly how I told you it happened. Then I asked if it was all right if I kept writing to her from the marines, and she said she didn't mind. Though she thought it wasn't a hot idea to think about her too much."

"It's probably not," I said.

"Not that I can help it," he said, and laughed. "I don't think she likes Rob much."

"Why do you say that?"

"I don't know. Just a feeling I get."

We came to the point in the road where it curved down into the valley, but Victor kept going over the curb and into the brush. I smelled the dusty creosote leaves and felt a drop of rain on my neck. Victor dug into his pants pocket and pulled out a little snub-nosed revolver.

"Then I asked her if she wanted this back," he said.

"Jesus. Where the hell did that come from?"

"Jess gave it to me for my birthday," he said, holding the gun on his flat, open palm. "She stole it from her stepdad's dresser." He laughed. "Don't look so surprised."

I was wondering what Rob would think about Jess stealing a gun from her stepdad. Probably he knew a little of what her life was like and felt he was saving her from that, or maybe it excited him that she was so unlike him. But my guess was it worried him. It might have been why he'd come to me about Victor, because he couldn't account for the fact that, before he'd known her, Jess had loved this other man who was so different from him. It seemed like something he'd have to think about tonight, and maybe for as long as he knew Jess.

Victor had gone deeper into the brush. "Check this out," he said, and took a small bullet out of his shirt pocket. "This is something Jess and I used to do out at Saguaro Lake." He put the bullet in the cylinder, flicked it shut, and brought his arm out, fully extended. "Shoot the moon," he said softly, and then the gun let out a sudden burst of flame, and the sound of a shot rang through the valley.

"You're crazy!" I shouted.

Victor gave me a serious look. "She'll have heard that," he said.

"She'll know what I did." Then he glanced up the street, where a lot of dogs had started barking, and said, "We better blaze."

We took off down the mountain, weaving between cholla and chaparral, the shale and gravel loose under our feet. Lights came on in houses around us, but soon we were far enough down the hill that I didn't worry about getting caught. It was good to be running with the rain on my face, Victor laughing beside me. I felt so good, in fact, as we ran down the dark foothills toward home, that I had to remind myself—and it was like a shock, like getting bad news—that I didn't even want to go there.

Ongchoma

──────

Lynn is taking her mother to the plastic surgeon's office in Tempe, driving west on McKellips, past industrial lots and fields of dry weeds. Her mother, a small, pretty woman in an owl-print blouse, folds and refolds a handkerchief in her lap as she stares out the window. Terrence, Lynn's roommate, sits in the backseat, leafing through a brochure on plastic surgery.

"Rhinoplasty, blepharoplasty, a little lipo," Terrence says, catching Lynn's eye in the rearview mirror. "In and out for only forty-five hundred bucks."

"Don't even think about it," Lynn says.

"Nothing major. Just touch-ups," he says. "I owe it to those I care about."

Terrence is thirty-seven and slender, with a straight long nose and the kind of dark, curling eyelashes Lynn wishes she had. He's three-quarters Indian and teaches Native American studies at Arizona State, where Lynn is an associate professor of comparative literature. He has come along today because he had a fight with his boyfriend, Cale, last night. Cale, twenty-six, a kickboxing instructor, came by at midnight, drunk and belligerent, and after a heated argument he punched Terrence three times below the right temple. Lynn heard it all from her bedroom. She called the police, but by the time they arrived Cale was long gone and Terrence wouldn't say anything about what had happened. Lynn stayed up with him until four in the morning, drinking Cuba Libres, watching Hedy Lamarr on the Movie Channel. By the time the sun brightened the windows, Terrence was laughing and seemed to have forgotten all about the fight.

They pass several dozen cement trucks, all lined up inside a chain-link fence. Behind them, a team of bulldozers raise a cloud of dust.

"So what are they building out there anyway?" Terrence asks, staring out the window. "It looks like the tenth circle of hell."

"It's a gravel quarry," Lynn says, "for cement. It's been like that since I was a kid."

"God," he says.

She can remember a miniature golf course near here—the brightly painted windmill and her brother, Nicky, slicing a putter through the air like a saber. She pictures her father scowling behind aviator sunglasses.

She has been thinking about her father all morning, partly because she knows he would not have approved of what her mother is about to do. There would have been no discussion of the matter, except for a few shouted injunctions. Lynn doesn't miss the man's military style or his occasional violent outbursts, but she does find something lacking in her life without him—his predictability, perhaps. After finishing her dissertation at Brown, Lynn took a position at Arizona State, and since then everything in her life has gone a little out of focus. She's abandoned a book on *The Decameron*, making her hopes for tenure thin at best. She can hardly remember a time when she was interested in Italian literature, or anything else for that matter. Lately she's even be-

gun to drink like one of her students—tequila poppers, kami-
kazes, and Jaegermeister shots—serious binges that run deep
into the evenings, so that her mornings are lost to a painful, protective haze. Terrence is usually her partner in crime, though she
drinks alone as well, in their house when he's away or at a local
bar among working-class men, some of whom she has gone home
with for the thrill of it. It's a way of finding the bottom, she thinks,
having done it before as an undergraduate. She fears she may
have already become an alcoholic. With the fall semester only a
few days away, she dreads having to get back to work. She's not
even sure she'll be able to do it.

On the left is the Salt River Canal, streams of beige water gush-
ing out of its floodgates. After turning south on Scottsdale Road,
they ease into Tempe. The streets are flanked by car dealerships
and hamburger stands. The Moose lodge sits at the back of an
oyster-shell lot. Beside it is the Elks lodge. Both have signs adver-
tising Friday Night Bingo.

"Do you think there's bad blood between the Elks and Mooses?"
Terrence asks, leaning over the front seat like a child on a trip.
"We should come out here some Friday night and see what goes
down."

"I used to go to the bingo at St. Mark's," Lynn's mother says,
"back when Larry and I moved to Phoenix."

"You know, Jeanette," Terrence says, "when your bandages
come off, we're having the biggest coming-out party of all time.
Black tie affair at the downtown Hilton. Twenty-piece band."

Jeanette smiles uneasily. She never knows when Terrence is
teasing her.

"I'm getting Engelbert Humperdinck to jump out of a cake and
sing 'You Must Have Been a Beautiful Baby.'"

Jeanette laughs in a relieved, girlish way.

They pass a storage facility called U-Store-It-Here, then a furniture warehouse with an enormous inflated gorilla on its roof.
The ape's outstretched arms joggle in a breeze. Beside a sporting
goods store, two teenagers make out on a strip of grass, the boy
on top, the girl holding his ass in both her hands.

"Ye gads," says Terrence, watching them slip away. "*Vive
l'amour.*"

The nurse at the plastic surgeon's office has what Terrence calls "The Personality." At least half the white women in Arizona have The Personality, he says. It is an amalgamation of mannerisms taken from daytime talk show hosts — stand-up comedy shtick, black sass, southern coquettishness. Terrence and Lynn have flipped through the channels during the day, tracing its origins.

"Listen, girl," the nurse says, wrapping a plastic ID bracelet around Jeanette's wrist, "this is so we don't lose you, *capice*?" She glances up at Terrence and Lynn, her eyes filled with a kind of willful attitude. Her skin has the puffy smoothness of too many laser peels. "I see you brought your gang along," she says.

"That's my daughter, Lynn," Jeanette says, "and her roommate, Terrence."

"Think she's ready to get beautiful?" the nurse asks them.

"She's *already* beautiful," Terrence says.

"Oh, I don't mean that," the nurse says, and for a moment The Personality vanishes into the air of the waiting room. She focuses on the bracelet, avoiding Terrence's gaze. "I just meant is she ready for Dr. Giles to enhance her *natural* beauty?" The phrase brings the glint back to her eye, and she stands up straight and cocks a hand on her hip. "I mean, happiness may be a woman's best cosmetic, but a little nip and tuck can't hurt."

"She had it bad," Terrence says as they walk across the parking lot.

An orange steam-cleaning truck makes its way between the rows of cars and SUVs, the operator a tired-looking teenage boy with livid acne. As they pass a wet strip where the truck has been, the ground smells sharp and dusty. A light-headed feeling comes over Lynn, so that for a moment her vision seems to brighten and blur.

"Your mother reminded me of a baby bird just now," Terrence says, moving beside her in his loping stride. "When I was a kid I found a little swallow behind our trailer and tried to nurse it back to health."

"Should I have tried to talk her out of it?" Lynn asks. She glances back at the small white clinic, where three of her mother's friends have had procedures already. All of them have emerged looking younger and well rested, a little unsettled by the attention they attract. Lately Lynn feels almost jealous of her mother, a pretty, cheerful woman who, in a couple of weeks, will be even prettier. Lynn can't imagine what *she'll* look like when she's sixty-two, especially if she keeps living the life she's been living. When she looks in the mirror, her features are vague and slightly unfamiliar, as if she's becoming another person altogether.

"So what happened to your little bird?" she asks Terrence.

"Don't ask," he says. "Birdie heaven. She'll be gorgeous, though, Lynn, I mean it. This isn't anything a thousand women don't go through every day."

They have somehow arrived at Lynn's car. She opens the door and lets the heat flood over her bare legs.

"Where to?" she asks.

Her mother will be in surgery for nearly four hours; after another two for recovery, she'll go to Lynn and Terrence's place in Tempe to recuperate for a few days.

"We could get a paper and check the movie listings," she says. "Or we could try to find a bookstore. Or we could just pop into the bar for a while."

"I love how casually you mention the bar," Terrence says, smiling, eyebrows raised. "As if we might go someplace else."

The bar is Pachinko's Tonga Room on University, a tiny clapboard place painted blue and green. Inside, a simulated-rock waterfall cools the air, and Lynn's eyes adjust to the dim light as she and Terrence take their usual places at the bar. The walls are festooned with fishing nets and captains' wheels; the scent of stale beer fills the air. Each time Lynn walks through the door the sound of dribbling water is like a promise of sedation, so that she feels elated immediately. Today she feels so good she almost orders a Diet Coke instead of her usual Cosmopolitan, but at the last minute she changes her order, then drinks the Cosmo quickly. Terrence orders a Chivas on the rocks, *his* usual. He lowers his head to the straw and doesn't look up until he's making slurping noises at the bottom of the glass. Lynn laughs, as she is meant to do. They order another round. The familiar slide goes through Lynn's body, a feeling she's come to anticipate these days. The place is empty except for the owner, who leans over the comics at the end of the bar, a thin man in a Polynesian shirt. His teeth, when he smiles, are crooked and yellow, like roots.

"I have the capacity for human kindness," Terrence says, swaying on his stool like a drunk in a TV movie. "I've got this capacity, don't you see? Don't you *see*?" He pounds the bar, trying to make Lynn laugh, trying to make her forget about Cale, who she asked about on the car ride over.

"You've got a capacity for human stupidity," she tells him.

He sips his drink and makes a sour face, ignoring her. "This tastes awful," he says. "Did you see him pour the Chivas?"

"He had the bottle," she says. "Who knows what was in it?" She fishes the maraschino cherry out of her glass and bites into it. "I'll stop bugging you," she says. "I know it's none of my business." She also knows that if she doesn't stop he'll bring up the men she's gone home with lately.

"Okay, but I'm through with him," Terrence says. He downs his drink and signals to the owner, who comes over and pours another round.

"I've got to call Stanley tomorrow," Lynn says. "He's left messages every day since Thursday."

"You ought to tape record that son of a bitch," Terrence says. "Take his ass to arbitration."

"Believe me, I've thought about it," she says.

"He's so quid pro quo it's not even funny."

Stanley Danillo is the Livingston-Daley Chair in the Comparative Literature Department. This summer, he's made several unsolicited advances toward Lynn, most of which fall within the definition of sexual harassment as outlined in the department handbook, *A Few Serious Words*. Lynn has actually considered doing what Terrence half-jokingly suggests—nailing Stanley's ass to the wall. His unwanted advances might be a way of advancing her career, which has no hope of advancing on its own. She's seen it happen: a suit is brought, and suddenly some ostensibly offended party has tenure. Of course, she could never jeopardize anyone else's career simply to further her own; and anyway she feels sorry for Stanley, a fifty-year-old arrested-development case who went through a messy divorce last fall. Lynn actually liked him before he started blowing the foul odor of collusion into his flirtations.

"Filing a suit could be my only chance of getting tenure," she says, testing the notion on Terrence.

"That's bullshit," he says. "You'll get tenure with or without that tub of lard."

"I won't."

"You *will*." But he has to look away at the dusty blowfish that hangs behind the bar. The fish is the color of parchment and riddled with holes, as if someone has shot it with a BB gun.

"I should never date bisexuals," Terrence says, abandoning her hopeless situation for his own.

Light shoots into the room as three men come through the back door. For a moment they appear as silhouettes against the brilliant day, then the door closes and they move around the dim back of the room, talking in aggressive voices. Lynn hears the musical sound of pool cues sliding from the rack. A country-western song comes on the jukebox. Terrence hunches over his drink. His entire presence seems to change when straight men are around.

Lynn hears footsteps and glances in the mirror behind the bar. A tall man is coming toward her, dressed in jeans and a nearly white denim work shirt. He leans on the counter and orders a pitcher of Schaeffer, the scent of cement and spicy aftershave coming off his body. He catches Lynn's eye before going back to a table.

"He likes you," Terrence says.

"He's unintentionally retro," she says. "He's got sideburns like Peter Fonda in *Easy Rider*."

"Good or bad?"

"Bad," she says, though she found the man attractive in a shabby way. When he caught her eye, she felt something shift within her. It's another feeling she's come to expect in her life: a subtle dilation, the physical manifestation of possibility. "They look like they work for the state," she says.

"I forgot you were so particular."

"Fuck off, Terrence."

Terrence grins, looking at the men in the mirror, watching them prowl around the pool table. Then his grin fades and he says, "Why do you think they don't respect me? Am I not wearing a shirt that shows the vein in my bicep?" He flexes his arm to show Lynn his vein. "You know I worked very hard to get this thing."

"What makes you think they don't respect you?"

"He checks you out like I'm not even here."

"You ought to learn tae kwon do," she says. "That way you could give him a quick roundhouse kick to the temple. And you could crack Cale's skull next time he tries to pull anything."

"I make Cale feel stupid," Terrence says. "That's why it happens. I goad him on."

"It can't be hard to make Cale feel stupid," she says.

"To be honest, I like it when he's mad," he says, smiling at the corners of his mouth. "Within reason, of course. It makes life more exciting. Not that you'd understand."

"That's the problem," she says. "I do understand."

In the back of the room, a man knocks a ball off the table and the other men laugh. When Lynn turns and looks, the one with sideburns winks at her.

"My father used to say, 'Never turn down a fuck,'" Terrence says, and gives a hard, dry laugh. "Can you imagine him saying that to me? He was talking about women, of course."

"Sensitive man."

"I had a horny family," Terrence says. "My sisters were always wandering off with reservation trash, getting pregnant, getting VD. My brothers made notches on their beds each time they fucked a girl, like World War II pilots."

"The opposite of my family."

"Oh, I can picture your family," he says, raising his chin and closing his eyes like a clairvoyant. "A dark figure sits at the head of the table. You and your mother are like two beautiful candles, waiting to be extinguished."

"That's close," she says. "Three beautiful candles. You're forgetting my brother."

"I wasn't thinking," Terrence says. "I'm sorry, kid."

"That's all right."

Lynn's little brother, Nicky, ran away when he was only seventeen. She's heard from him only one time since then — a postcard sent from San Francisco that said, "I'm fine. Tell him I'm starving."

"I was just thinking about Nicky this morning," she says. "He doesn't even know Dad died yet, I don't think."

"He should," Terrence says. "It would make a difference in his life. It's made a difference in mine."

In the mirror, the man with sideburns comes toward the bar, an empty pitcher in hand. Lynn tries hard not to glance at him but finally does. His eyes are on her.

"What's your name?" he asks.

"Rita Moreno." She keeps her eyes on the dusty bottles behind the bar.

"I'm Lyle."

"This is my husband, Chet," Lynn says, and puts a hand on Terrence's shoulder.

Terrence flashes her a look of panic before nodding at the man.

"You two're married?" The man laughs as if it's a joke he's still trying to figure out.

"Three years in June," she says.

The man's smile becomes mean: he doesn't believe her. He holds her gaze for a long moment, then says, "I come here Thursdays," and walks back to his friends.

One of the men in the back says, "Find something you like, Lyle?" and they all laugh.

Terrence shoots Lynn a mortified look, his shoulders hunched, his eyes wide and alert. "What a jerk," he whispers.

"No kidding," she says.

"You're wonderful, though. 'Rita Moreno.' God, I wish I were you."

───────────

It's the landscape that makes you want things, she thinks. They're driving west on University, past fenced-in wrecking yards and rows of rental equipment outlets. Camelback Mountain stands jagged and red against the endless sky. The light-headed feeling comes over Lynn again, so that she has to grip the wheel and concentrate hard on the road. It's a feeling almost like hyperventilation, as if she's breathed in too much of the bright blue sky.

She's thinking of the man at the bar, remembering the way his muscles rippled as he lifted his pitcher of beer. She'd like to go back and drink Long Island Iced Teas with him until the day gained the weight of inevitability. She's done it before. In one month she has gone home with four different men, all of them more like the sideburned man than anyone she ever dated in college. She finds it thrilling, because it's so unlike her, like smoking in the girls' room in junior high, catching a glimpse of her older, more daring self in the mirror, a cigarette in her mouth.

She likes the way the men's eyes shift from arrogance to fear as she flirts with them. They're not used to educated women, and this allows her to keep them on edge. In their homes, she takes in their mismatched furniture, their tangled bed sheets, feeling a little like an anthropologist. She often experiences a yearning tenderness for the men but keeps it inside at all times. She has been frightened more than once, but so far nothing awful has happened, aside from the time when a broad-shouldered mechanic pushed her face into a pillow. He let go as soon as she screamed. "No offense," he said, embarrassed and a little petulant, "but I thought you'd like it like that." She carries a can of Mace in her purse and thinks of it from time to time, when a man is rolling over her in bed, when all his weight is suddenly upon her.

They stop by the university to pick up schedules for the fall semester, then, with time on their hands, go home to prepare the guest room for Lynn's mother.

For the past year they have rented a single-story ranch-style house at the end of a cul-de-sac. On the roof is a faded plastic Santa Claus, discovered by Terrence at a yard sale several weeks ago. Already four neighbors have complained about it, but Terrence keeps forgetting to take it down. He looks at it with guilty eyes each time they come home.

In the living room the blinds are drawn. Lynn goes to the extra room and makes up the little bed for her mother. When she comes out, Terrence is on the sofa with a beer in each hand. On the glass coffee table is a sandpainting he did four nights ago, a depiction of an Indian creation myth. Three elongated stick figures stand in a circle: First Man, First Woman, and Coyote, the trickster/creator. Coyote has just stolen a child of the monster Tieholtsodi, a mistake that will keep First Man and First Woman on the run for many years, moving up from one spoiled world to the next, hoping to finding a home. Terrence started sandpainting six months ago, and his paintings are already as clean and accomplished as the ones Lynn has seen at the National Museum of the American Indian.

She leans over the painting, breathing in its earth scent. She loves its burnt siennas, its antelope browns. "It's your best one yet," she says.

Terrence gives it a disapproving look, his lips pressed into a line.

She is always surprised by his serious side, especially when it comes to his Native American heritage. He rarely talks about it. She'll read an article that he's written on U.S.-tribal relations and be amazed by the depth of emotion he brings to the material. He has received a governor's grant for his photo essay, *Bring Me Your Saddest Arizona*, a collection of black-and-white photographs chronicling the confrontation between Sonoran desert and suburban landscape. Lately he has become disenchanted with teaching, partly because enrollment in his courses has dropped, partly because of the increasingly hermetic nature of the Native American Studies Department. After six years, he's tired of seeing the brightest Indian students focus only on Native American studies. He'd like them to be leaders of the community, of the world, not just of the department, where his colleagues are mostly small-minded and distrustful of outsiders. His feelings are considered scandalous — even among some of his students. Last year, he told a class of graduate students that he had no Indian blood at all, and a few of them glared at him all semester. "They wanted to scalp me," he told Lynn. "It was too stupid. I used to be proud of what I do."

Lynn sips her beer and leafs through a stack of mail from the department — offers for free textbooks, class lists for the three sections she'll teach this quarter. At the bottom of the pile is a note from Stanley Danillo, handwritten on department letterhead. "Lynn," it reads. "You ought to come up to the house on

Friday and have a sturgeon steak. I caught three big beauties off the Florida Keys, and they're dying to get BBQ'ed! Also an exciting little bottle of Sancerre! And, for breakfast, fresh blueberries! (Wink, wink.) We can talk about your work if you like. Best, Stanley."

She almost gives the note to Terrence, so that the two of them can groan about it, but in the end she doesn't. Is she actually thinking of going to Stanley's? Or does she see the note as what it might become: documentation in a harassment suit? Could she actually *do* that to the man? She's been to Stanley's for department gatherings and, gazing at the high-ceilinged rooms and the original art on the walls, has thought how wrong it is that he should have so much while she has so little.

These thoughts have always vanished once she's out the door, but they're back now, in her own shabby living room, feeling like the purest, nascent bloom of possibility. She folds the note three times and puts it in her purse.

It is late afternoon when they pull into the clinic parking lot. Lynn and Terrence take the elevator to the third floor and wait a few minutes before Jeanette is brought out in a wheelchair, tiny and bandaged, her face encircled by gauze. Her skin, from forehead to chin, is as pink and shiny as a blister. Dots of blood show at the corners of her mouth. She has the slow, heavy-lidded gaze of a newborn child.

"Mom?" Lynn says.

Jeanette glances around as if searching for some lost object.

"She's blotto," the nurse says, smiling. "She'll probably zonk right out on the way home."

"Why is she bleeding?" Lynn asks.

"It's pretty standard. It means Dr. Giles went deep with the laser, which is good, actually. She got a lot of bang for her buck."

Lynn's mother looks up with a concerned expression on her face. ". . . tight," she says, and touches the bandage where it cuts into her jaw.

"Don't touch, Jeanette," the nurse says.

"Can't they loosen the bandage?" Lynn asks.

"I'm afraid they can't," the nurse says. "It has to be tight to protect the stitches."

Lynn's mother says something else, glancing at Lynn with a timid, hopeful smile on her face.

"What, Mom?" Lynn says.

"How do I look?" she asks.

"Poor thing," Terrence says, as they ride east on Apache Boulevard. He's watching Lynn's mother sleep in the backseat, her head rocking against the window. "She'll be our little child," he says. "We'll raise her up the best we know how."

Lynn turns on Alhambra, passes the high school. On their own street she slows for three boys on skateboards, all of them shirtless, horrendous tattoos banding their arms. Terrence frowns at the Santa Claus as she bumps into their driveway. Lynn's mother sits up in the back and brings a hand to her cheek.

"No, no, Ma. You can't touch it." Lynn gets out and helps her mother out of the back. It makes her think of trips they made to the drive-in when she was a child — falling asleep, then waking as her father carried her to the house.

Inside, Terrence goes to the spare room to turn down the covers on the little twin bed. Lynn leads her mother through the living room, matching her tiny, childlike steps. Halfway there, Jeanette veers toward Terrence's sandpainting. "Oh, beautiful," she says. "Look." She leans over the table. "I've got to get back to my paintings. Do you remember my paintings?"

"Of course, Ma," Lynn says. "They were great."

Lynn's mother painted for a few years after Lynn's father died — landscapes and still lifes of fruits and vegetables. Lynn was surprised by how talented she was.

Her mother beams, apparently imagining herself at the easel. Then she allows Lynn to guide her to the guest room. Her button-down blouse is easy to remove. She's brought a loose cotton nightgown and slippers. Naked, her body is as small and delicate as a girl's. In the bed she lies still while Lynn places pillows on both sides of her to keep her from rolling over in the night.

"You all right?" Lynn asks.

"Snug as a bug in a rug," she says.

"It's peaceful having her here," Terrence says. He is lying beside Lynn on the living-room floor, a half-full brandy snifter resting on his sternum. "Don't you feel as if your life has meaning now?"

"Suddenly, yes," she says. "It's what I've been waiting for all these years."

She feels as if her mother is still in danger, though of course there's no reason to think so. The surgery was elective, routine; her recovery is a matter of course. Perhaps it is the betrayal of Lynn's father that worries her. In his life he made them all fear betraying him. Lynn wonders if her mother's surgery is a sign of her liberation, and hopes it is. She wonders when her own liberation will take place.

"Do you know what I want to do tonight?" Terrence asks. "Do you know what I would really love to do?"

"What?"

"Anything but finish this brandy and pass out on the floor."

"I like your attitude," she says. "Aim high."

"We're living on borrowed time," he says, and the humor drains from his face. He sets his snifter on the floor. "For some reason today just seemed like the end of the summer."

"I dread teaching again," she says.

"I'm not getting back together with Cale," he says. "Earlier, when I said I wouldn't, I thought I would. I was lying. But I can't. I haven't got the strength anymore." He smiles in a way that makes her think he'll cry, but instead he scoots over the floor toward her. The melon scent of his styling gel fills the air. He gives Lynn a quick peck on the cheek, then he keeps pecking her until she laughs. "You don't mind, do you?" he asks.

"I don't mind at all," she says, though in a moment a pounding comes to her chest. "Have you ever kissed a girl before?"

"Oh, sure," he says. "I've kissed lots of them. I had four girlfriends in high school."

"When did you know you were gay?" she asks.

"Long before that. I was hoping I wasn't, of course."

"So what were they like? Your girlfriends?"

"Not as smart as you. Not as sexy." He looks at her in a plainly appreciative way. "Not as blessed with your certain *je ne sais quoi*."

"You're too kind," she says.

"Do you know I've wanted to kiss you ever since today at Pachinko's?"

"Shut up."

"I'm serious." He gives her a devilish look.

"You're drunk," she says.

"It was that jerk at the bar, I think. The way he wanted you so badly. The way you handled yourself. I think I fell a little in love with you at Pachinko's."

"That's ridiculous."

"I'm kissing you for real, okay?" He sits up, pretending to reel backward as he did at the bar. But he scoots over and, holding her face in both hands, kisses her on the mouth, his lips parted. Lynn's veins flood with adrenaline. Little by little the feeling becomes comfortable, like wading into cool water that eventually comes to seem warm. She wraps her arms around his neck.

"I want to make love to you," he says.

"That's crazy," she says, and feels half crazy herself.

"I want to, though. I keep thinking of being in bed with you after we've done it, basking in the afterglow." He rolls off of her and lets out a sigh. "God, I am crazy," he says. "I'm sorry, Lynn. I'm sorry if I'm being unusual."

"You're definitely being that." She props herself up on an elbow. "I'm flattered, though." She takes a sip of brandy and holds it in her mouth until it burns. "Would you even enjoy it?"

"I'm pretty sure I would," he says, grinning.

"Now we're both going crazy," she says.

"Why? Are you thinking about it, too?" His face lights up.

She doesn't answer. She's trying to remember which panties she put on this morning. She wonders whether there are condoms in her bedside drawer. She feels that if she remains quiet for a while they'll both start laughing. But the moment for laughing comes and goes.

"We'll go to my room," she says. "I don't want my mom to hear anything."

"We'll be quiet as little church mice," he says, rising to his knees.

In the light from the kitchen, he looks like a man about to jump from a high cliff into shallow water. She takes his hand and leads him down to the end of the hall, where they kiss against the doorjamb. They are just stepping into the bedroom when a knock comes at the front door — a startling sound, five raps in a row. Terrence goes as still as a heron.

"We don't have to answer it," she says.

"You're right," he says, relieved.

But Cale has his own key, and Lynn hears it jingle before it slides into the door lock. She and Terrence rush back to the living room and pick up their snifters. They are in comically nonchalant positions when Cale comes in, like guests at a cocktail party that has suddenly vanished.

"What's going on?" Cale asks, glancing from Lynn to Terrence, his eyes thin and suspicious. "You guys wasted again?"

"No, but *you* probably are," Terrence says. He walks casually to the couch, sits down, and opens a magazine.

"Yeah, right," Cale says. He scans the room as if looking for clues. He's a small, muscular man with close-cropped, bleached-white hair. He goes into the kitchen, and Lynn hears the fridge door open and close. When he comes out he has a bottle of beer in his hand.

"This is the first drink I've had all day," he says, a little sadly, as if he expects them to feel sorry for him. "I taught lessons since eight this morning."

"No one said you could come in here," Terrence says, flipping a magazine page.

"No one asked," Cale says. "Hey, let's go out. I want to talk to you."

"I don't want to talk to *you*." Terrence turns another page.

Cale sighs, glancing at Lynn. "Don't you have someplace to be, honey? I know how much you love to eavesdrop, but we could use a minute here."

"Fuck off," she says, and goes into the kitchen. She rinses her snifter and pours a glass of water. Through the window she sees two girls across the street, both of them smoking cigarettes. One has bright green hair. The other wears a T-shirt that says DEAD AS ANYTHING. Lynn hears Cale in the living room, his voice sharp and full of potential harm. It reminds her of her father's voice in the days before Nicky ran away.

"Don't tell me I don't feel bad," Cale is saying. "How do you know what I feel?"

"I don't care how you feel," Terrence says. "It doesn't matter anymore."

"Don't *be* like that." The floorboards groan as Cale crosses the room. "And put down that fucking magazine!"

Lynn walks out as Cale is leaning over the couch, yanking the magazine out of Terrence's hands. He turns and sees her. His face breaks into a grin.

"Did you see that, Lynnie? I wrinkled this magazine. You gonna call the cops now?"

"I might."

"I'll call them," Terrence says, standing from the couch. He reaches for the phone, but Cale shoves him hard in the back, knocking him into the coffee table. The sandpainting is shaken into a blur of brown. Terrence stares at it.

"It's not *my* fault," Cale says. "You did it."

Terrence tries to pick up the phone again, but this time Cale slaps it so hard it flies out of his hands and smacks the wall. Cale assumes a martial-arts pose, legs apart, arms held away from his body.

"You *ass*hole," Terrence says.

Lynn rushes into her bedroom. She picks up her own phone and begins to dial 911, then sees her purse on the bed. She hangs up, reaches into the purse and feels the Mace can, heavy and cool. She takes it out, removes the cap, and walks into the living room.

"Get out of here," she says, pointing the can at Cale.

Cale huffs a laugh, glancing around as if everyone might laugh with him. His earring flashes in the light from the kitchen. "What are you going to do, Lynnie? Mace me?"

"I will," she says, "if you don't leave right now."

He takes a step toward her, and she squeezes the nozzle. It is almost too easy, a quick squeeze and Cale is buckling to his knees, his palms flying to his face. "Shit, shit!" he says, pressing his shoulder against the floor. He writhes, boots knocking the bookcase, books and knickknacks tumbling from the shelves. "You fucking bitch!" he screams.

Terrence comes over and looks at him. "It can't hurt *that* bad," he says. "She barely got you."

"Why did you fucking *do* that?" Cale shouts, kicking the wall, searching for Lynn with his blood-colored eyes.

Lynn is a little surprised herself. She feels a surge of pity for Cale as he wiggles around, cheeks slick with mucus, face red as cooked crab. He coughs and sniffs and says quietly, almost to himself, "This is such bullshit."

Terrence looks at Lynn. She can see disgust in his eyes and hopes it is intended for Cale, not for her. She feels as if she deserves it.

"I'll take him out to the hose," Terrence says, lifting Cale up by the collar. Cale rises to all fours and lets Terrence lead him out the door like a dog.

Lynn follows them onto the lawn. The night is warm; the street sparkles like mica in the moonlight. Terrence turns on the water spigot and drags the hose over the lawn. "Don't expect me to feel sorry for you," he says to Cale.

Cale brings the water to his face, letting it run down his chest and darken his T-shirt. He holds the end of the hose to one eye, then the other, then catches his breath. "She's crazy," he says. "I didn't even *do* anything."

"You're the one who's crazy," Terrence says, glancing up at Lynn, shaking his head.

"Why? What did I do?" Cale whines, a child wrongly scolded. "Why are you *being* like this?"

Lynn goes back into the house. She knows there's nothing she can do now. If he is able to, Cale will convince Terrence to go out for a drink and then persuade him to make up. If Terrence refuses, Cale may become violent again. Lynn can only hope Terrence has the strength to keep the promise he made to her. She doesn't know if she could do it under similar circumstances.

Inside, Lynn's mother is standing in the living room, her yellow nightgown aglow in the light from the kitchen.

"I heard a noise," she says, looking dazed. "For a minute I thought it was your father."

"Oh, Mom," Lynn says. She hugs Jeanette and leads her down the hall. "It was just a friend of Terrence's. It's over now."

In the guest room, tiny glow-in-the-dark stars illuminate the ceiling. Lynn's mother climbs into bed and, seeing the stars, says, "Oh, look at that, Lynn. Stars." She beams at Lynn, then her smile fades and she says, "In my dream Nicky was fighting with your father. Do you ever dream about Nicky?"

"Of course," Lynn says, "all the time."

"I do, too." Her voice is low and distant, as if she's gone back to the dream. "Usually, in my dreams, he comes home and everything's fine. Not in this one, though."

"Things are going to be fine now," Lynn says, and as the words come out she can almost believe they're true.

Terrence is on the couch when she comes back to the living room. The front door is shut. Cale is nowhere in sight. Terrence's expression is that of a young fireman who's come out of a burning building. He has picked up the pieces of a broken kachina doll and laid them on the coffee table. There is a red body, a thick yellow arm, a large blue pill-shaped head.

"I hope it can be fixed," she says, taking the body into her hands.

"Me too," he says. "That's Ongchoma. He's one of my favorites. They call him the compassionate kachina."

"I don't know anything about him."

"When we were kids, we had a thing called the Powamuya Ceremony," he says. "There's a part in it where the kids get whipped with yucca fronds—it's supposed to teach you something about the roughness of life. It stings like hell. Anyway, we were supposed to imagine Ongchoma touching us with mano, this salve, and making us feel better."

"Did it work?"

"Not really." He grins. "But it was nice to be able to think of him, someone trying to help. I still think of him sometimes. He's a good old guy, with his big old head."

She lays the body on the table. "I wish I hadn't sprayed Cale," she says. "It was overboard."

"Don't be stupid," he says. "I only wish I'd done it."

"Do you really?"

"Of course," he says.

She is surprised by how much she has come to rely on him these last few months without ever really noticing it. She wants to tell him about Stanley now, to take the note out of her purse and let him read it, to see his reaction when she tells him what she planned to do. But they have been through enough drama for one day. Maybe she will tell him in the morning.

"How's Cale?" she asks.

"A little snotty, but he'll clean up all right."

"I'm sorry about your painting," she says, leaning over it. She can just make out the forms of First Man and First Woman. They look like ghostly figures coming through a dust storm.

"They're not supposed to last," he says. "You offer them as a kind of prayer, then mess them up. I did this one for you, actually."

"Why?" she asks.

"Because I like you."

"Even though I'm a drunken bitch?"

"Especially because you're a drunken bitch." He smiles, raising his eyebrows. "I don't suppose we'll make love now, huh? Weren't we about to hop in the sack or something?"

"Were we?" she asks, and they both laugh.

"You don't have ants in your pants, do you? That's what my sisters used to call it. When they got turned on and couldn't— you know. For guys, of course, it was the Blue Balls." He makes a grave face.

"I don't have ants in my pants," she says.

"That's good," he says. "I don't think I have the Blue Balls. You know what we ought to do, though?"

"What?"

"We ought to pretend we've made love already. We could just go to bed and lie there in the afterglow."

"Sounds like a nice idea," she says.

She is happy to take his hand and follow him down the hall-way, which is cool and smells of her mother's bandages. Lynn's room is dark, and the steady whir of the air conditioner comes through the wall. Somewhere in the neighborhood a dog barks three times in a row. Lynn pulls down the covers and slides into the bed, feeling the cool sheets against her legs. Terrence slides in beside her. His weight makes the bedsprings sing.

"So now we're here in the afterglow," he says, and she can hear in his voice that he's smiling. He takes her hand under the sheet.

"That's right," she says. "And we've got our little child in a room just down the hall, and we have to take good care of her."

"And I'm a construction worker," he says in a low, oaky voice. "I have to get up butt-ass early in the morning and build houses. I have to work very hard to support our family."

"We have fun, though," she says. "We've got a nice pop-up camper that we take to Sedona on the weekends."

"And you have The Personality," Terrence says.

Lynn laughs. "And you have a big gut just like Stanley Danillo."

"And our life," he says, "is simple and good."

Between
Tubac and
Tumacacori

I followed the directions to Mullin's house, through a neighborhood of packed-dirt yards and low stucco houses. Kids were setting off firecrackers on one of the streets, and there were battered old couches and chairs in the yards, with people sitting out under the streetlights, drinking beer. Mullin lived on a street called Ocotillo, in a small yellow cottage with gravel in the yard. I'd never been to the house before. His girl-friend came out as I pulled to the curb. She squinted at my car like she wanted me to turn around and go back where I'd come from.

"I'm Boone," I called through the passenger window. "You must be Sandy."

"Mullin's not here," she said.

"Any idea how long he'll be?" I asked.

"Hour or two."

"You don't mind if I just use your bathroom, do you? It's been a long drive from Tempe." I gave her a big smile, but she just looked at me in a disapproving way, then turned and went into the house. Since she'd left the door open, I followed her in.

The place was bad inside — dirty brown carpet and fake-wood paneling, everything dark as a mine. Toys and clothes lay scattered across the living-room floor, and there were bits of cereal and crackers in the carpet around the dining table. Over the sofa they had a couple of seascape paintings like you see in cheap motels. They cheered things up about as well as you'd imagine.

"Bathroom's down the hall," she said. "If I smell heroin cooking in there I'll call the cops."

I had to laugh at that. "What makes you think you'd smell heroin?"

"I'm not stupid," she said, and walked with determination into the kitchen, where I heard the faucet go on and dishes rattle in the sink.

I shouldn't have expected her to like me. Mullin and I had met at Dobbins State Prison five years before and had worked for a while at a federal program laying water lines in Wickenburg. But mostly we'd dealt drugs in the time we'd known each other, heroin and speed, which we'd bought from a middle-aged Nicaraguan woman named Claudia Paz in South Tucson. Our customers were U of A students and workers at the air force base, and we lived in a little two-bedroom house by the university, where we had a lot of crazy times, though I was always careful about the heroin. It was Mullin's personality that he couldn't leave it alone for a few days in between, and in the end that was what split us up — me nagging all the time and him not even wanting to kick, though there were other problems as well, like the fact that he thought he could run the whole show and treat me like some kind of employee.

It might have been why I'd come all the way out here to deliver the money I owed him even though I could have sent it in the mail — because I wanted to show him I'd done all right on my own, had prospered, even, in ways I wouldn't have if he'd been around. But there's always something wrong with your plans if you bother to make them, and with Mullin half the time it was a woman who was trying to clean him up. The other half it was the fact that he was in love with himself.

She was at the dining table when I came out, wearing a pair of black-framed glasses, leaning over a textbook.

"What're you working on?" I asked, because I wanted to be nice. I wanted us to be getting along when Mullin arrived.

"Accounting," she said, and kept her eyes on the book.

"Mullin said you worked at the Kalil plant. You quit that?"

"I work there in the day," she said. "At night I take classes."

"Must be hard."

She glanced up. Her eyes were green, the color of the old 7Up bottles, with bits of brown mixed in. She had the pitted cheeks you see on users sometimes. I thought that was why she was uptight about the heroin, because she'd had troubles of her own. She was looking at me when a voice came from down the hall, and we both turned around.

A child had come into the hallway, a little towheaded boy of eight or nine. He wore a striped pajama top and was naked underneath. His eyes were the same dark green as Sandy's.

"Marky," she said, and went over to him. "What's the matter, honey? Where's your 'jama bottoms at?"

The way he stared at me with his big green eyes made me think of my brother, Alex, who has Down's syndrome. This kid didn't have that kind of face, though.

Sandy led him down the hall. I heard them talking in one of the rooms —Sandy saying, "Couldn't you sleep, baby?" and then the kid's voice, which was drawn out and round, like Alex's, so that I couldn't make out the words.

She came back and started reading again.

"He all right?" I asked.

"Course he's all right," she said. "He just woke up, is all."

"The only reason I ask is that my little brother has Down's syndrome. My brother, Alex."

She gave me a distrustful look.

"Not that I'm saying that's what's wrong with your son," I said. "I can see it isn't. He doesn't have that flat face."

"How old is your brother?" she asked.

"Nineteen. He's a big kid, looks like a goddamn linebacker or something."

A smile played across her face, but then she was serious again. "Mark nearly drowned when he was two and a half. It affected his brain."

"I'm sorry to hear it," I said.

"There's nothing to be sorry about. He's just started a new school this last month. He does very well."

"My brother's in the Stepping Stones program. You heard of that?"

"I have," she said. "I've heard it's good."

"He likes it a lot."

She glanced at the book as if remembering it was there, then said, "Look, I've got an exam tomorrow. If I don't do well I'll fail the class, and it's a class I've taken once already. I can't afford to take it again."

"That's all right. I'll just sit over here and wait. I won't bother you anymore."

"I have to work hard to get where I'm going," she said in a kind of apologetic way.

"Forget it," I said.

"Mullin's usually home by ten. It shouldn't be much longer. I'm from Kentucky, and I'm usually more hospitable than this. I'm sorry I was rude when you arrived."

"No worries. You don't know me from Adam."

"Actually, I feel like I know you pretty well." She was looking at me closely. "Mullin's told me a lot about you."

"That's probably why you were rude," I said.

She laughed.

"I was never strung out, though," I said. " I have to insist upon that. If Mullin told you I was, he was lying."

"Well, Mullin doesn't always get the truth just right, does he?"

"No, he doesn't. I was the one trying to get *him* cleaned up."

"He did say that," she said. "Actually, he told me you were the best friend he's ever had." Her eyes were still on me, frank and even. "He's told me a lot about being in prison. More than you might expect. He said you two were quite a pair when you were there."

"I suppose we were," I said.

"He said you were about as close as two men can be."

"What's that supposed to mean?"

"Should it mean something?" she asked.

"It doesn't to me."

"All right, then," she said. "It doesn't to me either."

I laughed, there was so much built-up tension in the room. I was trying to figure out what she knew about Dobbins, or whether she knew anything at all. She might have just been trying to make me tell her what went on, the way people do. I couldn't imagine why Mullin would say anything about it.

"I thought you had to study," I said.

"That's right, I should get back to work."

"Okay, then," I said.

It was funny. I'd started to like her, and I think she liked me too, but at the same time we were suspicious of each other. She glanced at the book as if considering the possibility of getting any work done with me around, then she stood and said, "I think I'll study in my room for a while. You don't mind waiting for Mullin alone, do you? I wouldn't imagine you'd take anything of ours."

"I don't see much worth taking," I said.

"That might be true," she said, looking at me in a bitter way, as if she were sorry she'd bothered to talk to me in the first place.

After she'd gone, I went out and smoked a cigarette, standing by my car in the warm air, listening to the trill of a nighthawk. Did she really know what went on at Dobbins? I couldn't see why Mullin would tell her about it. Maybe he'd spoken aloud in a dream or let it out when he was drunk once. I considered shooting up — I was getting that draw in my chest — but I wanted to be straight when Mullin came home, so I went back inside. There were beers in the fridge, and I drank one, leaning against the counter, checking out the pictures on the fridge door. There was one of Mullin on an old Yamaha bike, laughing at something that had happened out of the frame. He looked the same as always, tall and lean, a cocky grin on his face. There was a shot of him with Sandy and the boy, all of them dressed in swimsuits, standing on the bank of some muddy river. Below the photos was a xeroxed paper with the words "THE PROMISE" at the top. Underneath, it said:

We promise to be Committed under Christ to Sharing
our Lives, to Improving our Mutual Bond,
and to walking the Path
toward the Fulfillment of Dreams.

They had both signed it at the bottom. I read it a couple of times, then took it down and read it again, then folded it and put it in my pocket. The more I thought about Sandy, the madder I was at her for bringing up the Dobbins thing, because here I was thinking about something I'd nearly forgotten. I took the paper out of my pocket, but it was too wrinkled to put on the fridge again, so I just crumpled it up and threw it in the garbage.

I went into the living room and watched MTV, which was showing old heavy-metal videos. They made me think about my brother, Alex, who always liked metal and would rock out whenever I put it on the stereo. He used to have long hair and would whip it around like Angus Young and make devil horns with his hands. It always cracked me up.

Alex had hardly recognized me the last time I was home, had just stared at me like I was a stranger. I gave him the rock salute, but he didn't seem to know what it meant anymore. He'd grown four inches and was much bigger, a hundred and ninety pounds.

His hair was cut in the same square way as Uncle Philip's, who was living with them at the time.

By the time Mullin got home I'd nearly fallen asleep watching TV. I heard his bike in the driveway, a high-pitched whine, then his footsteps coming up the drive. It was surprising to see him walk through the door, tan and wearing new-looking jeans. He seemed a little uneasy, though he was grinning in the old Mullin way.

"Looks like somebody finally got a decent set of wheels," he said, and jerked a thumb at the window.

"You like that?" I went over and looked at my car in the drive, a '67 Firebird, built the year I was born. I'd bought it three months before from a software engineer in Apache Junction. "Hey, what're you riding these days?" I asked. "That bike sounded suspiciously Japanese."

"Yeah, just a Yamaha," he said, shrugging. "Gets me around, though."

A dog barked somewhere in the neighborhood. I heard the toilet flush down the hall and thought Sandy might come into the room, but she didn't.

"So how're things?" Mullin asked.

"Real good," I said. "I'm on an upswing. I found some work out by ASU, these kids I met through Hohner. It's a good situation, a lot of college kids with cash on their hands. Beautiful girls. It's a clientele that didn't exist a few years ago."

"Well, good for you, Boone." He went into the kitchen to get a beer. I saw him glance at the fridge as if he'd noticed the xeroxed paper was missing.

"Sandy go to bed?" he asked.

"About an hour ago."

"You two get a chance to talk?"

"A bit," I said. "She was studying for a test, though."

"She's trying to get a bookkeeper's license," he said. "Get a decent job."

"Sounds like a good idea. Hey, speaking of which, I got your money." I took a wad of twenties out of my pocket and handed it to him. "Sorry it took so long."

"Don't worry about it. It was me who took off. I can't bitch."

"That's true." I went over and looked at my car again. "Fuck, this feels good," I said. "I don't owe anybody any money right now. I'm in the clear."

"That's great, Boone."

"A nice car, a place to stay. Money coming in."

"Good for you, man."

"Course, I'm always looking for a partner," I said, and smiled like it might be a joke. "If you know anyone who might be interested."

Mullin shook his head. "It ain't me," he said. "I appreciate your asking, though."

"I didn't say you. I just said if you know someone."

"No, I don't think so." He had to pretend to think for a while. "Not offhand."

"You're pretty happy with what you got going here, I guess."

He glanced around the awful room, which made me feel bad for him. But he managed to nod and say, "I like where I'm at in my head, you know? That's the main thing for me these days."

"Fair enough," I said. "Well, I'm meeting a guy I know in Nogales, this guy Mako. I got to drive all the way back in the morning."

"What're you getting in Nogales?"

"What do you think?"

"No, I mean — I was wondering if you'll get any meth. I've been working long hours. I could use some help staying awake." He gave a little shrug like it was no big deal. He couldn't meet my eye, though.

"This guy'll have meth, sure."

"Just if you get it," he said.

"You'll be here tomorrow?"

"Right there on the couch," he said. "It's my day off." He gave me the old Mullin grin.

"Good to see you, bro," I said, and shook his hand.

"You too," he said, but he still couldn't meet my eye.

I stopped off at a Bob's Big Boy and ordered a Sprite, then shot up in the bathroom and got back on the highway. It was a pleasure just to be in my car with loud music on the stereo and the desert going past. I was glad Mullin hadn't come along and could hardly believe I'd asked him in the first place, because if he *had* come I knew it'd only be a few weeks before he'd be running the show again and I'd just be some little dog trotting along behind him. And then six or seven months down the road he'd split, and I'd feel like hell about it.

It was true we'd been through a lot together — being in Dobbins and getting in tight spots there and afterward — and things *had* happened between us, because that's the way it is in prison, though it doesn't necessarily mean anything once you're on the outside.

The only time it was ever an issue was when we were camping once up by Sedona, about a month after I got out of jail. We had our girlfriends with us — it was a party trip, our trunk filled with two cases of beer and ice. We'd gone off to gather some firewood, Mullin and me, and were walking through a wooded glen. We were both pretty wasted. Mullin was messing with his flashlight, shining it up at his chin to make his face look red, and then the next thing I knew he'd dropped the flashlight and was hugging me and kissing me on the mouth. I struggled at first, trying to push him away, but then I just sort of went with it. There was something brave about it, something frightening and real, because we weren't at Dobbins anymore. I had my eyes open and was looking at a little scrub bush that was lit up by the flashlight. I didn't know why I was letting Mullin kiss me; it wasn't what I'd wanted. And even if it could have been right — like if we were both completely different people — it was all of it his idea, not my own. I was glad when he just started laughing and we could both pretend it had never happened.

On the highway there were no cars, just the tiny lights of houses way off in the distance, where you'd have to be crazy to live. I passed Tubac and Tumacacori, both quiet and black, then Nogales, with its bars and motels and seedy little strip clubs. I eased off the highway and cut through town, passing rows of low clapboard houses. There were Mexican families sitting around tables, eating. I thought about Alex, back home with Mom and Uncle Philip, eating his pepper steaks and macaroni and cheese, his favorite meal, wearing his Raiders T-shirt. He's a Raiders fan now instead of a metal-head, which is Uncle Philip's influence. I thought about the time I took him to the Judas Priest show at Veterans' Memorial. Then I thought of the time he fell off the roof, which I always ended up thinking about late at night when I was alone.

We'd gone up there like we always did. I'd gotten him stoned by blowing smoke in his face, which was something I did from time to time. Alex loved to get stoned, and I couldn't see any harm in it, given what was already wrong with him. Mom was at work, and we were just listening to tapes, waiting to get hot enough to jump in the pool. Then I went to turn up the boom box, and Alex fell off the roof. I didn't even hear a sound until his body smacked the concrete.

Afterward he told Mom I'd pushed him. I didn't know why. It might have been his way of saying it was my fault, which was true, I admit — getting him stoned and being too stoned myself to watch him like I should have. But I never would have pushed him.

Mom said she believed me, but later she said something that made me wonder. We were at the hospital, waiting for Alex to get his X rays back, and she said, "He can just make you so desperate sometimes. We've given up our lives for him." She was trying to make me feel better, I know, but it was the kind of thing you'd say to someone who'd actually pushed his brother off the roof, and I never forgot that. Mom had been desperate with Alex a hundred times and had smacked him once or twice. But I didn't feel like I'd given up anything for him. He could be difficult. You had to do things just like he was used to, following the bedtime ritual, saying certain things at just the right times. If you gave him an irregular-shaped cookie or even moved one of his toys from where he kept it in his room, he could go into a tantrum. But he was in better shape than a lot of the kids at Stepping Stones, and we always got on well. He liked to say, "Boone's way cool!" and "Party on, Boone!" If anything, I wish I'd given up *more* — stayed and tried to be a better brother.

Alex was different after he fell, frightened around me, as if he thought I meant to do him harm. He eventually got to where he'd listen to music with me like in the old days, but it was never quite the same. It wasn't long after he fell that I left home and got an apartment near the junior college.

I took a job at the Cudahy plant and signed up for some college classes, but after a couple of months I started selling weed and got arrested for that, then got busted selling blotter acid, which is where they get you with the weight laws. They put me in the state penitentiary, and I met Mullin there. It was definitely a place where you needed a friend, and Mullin was a good one to have, since he'd learned a lot in the month he'd already served. We got tight in a hurry and stayed that way. When we got out at around the same time, we just went on from there.

It was eleven o'clock when I got to Mako's. He was on his leather couch, rolling a joint, listening to the Scorpions on a Bang and Olufsen stereo he'd just bought. He was a good guy, Mako, this three-hundred-pound Samoan with a gold front tooth and a tattoo of a gecko on his neck. He was always happy to see me and would give me some tequila or single-malt scotch, and more often than not I'd just crash at his place to save me the drive back to Tempe. Sometimes we'd end up watching some pretty hard-core pornos he ordered through the mail, and he'd get all into them, laughing when the women got hurt or calling them bitches or whatever, but I always thought he was a decent guy and would never try to hurt anyone. I'd seen him with his grandma when she lived with him for a while, this little raisin-faced woman. Mako cooked her meals and gave her baths, and when anyone came over he'd wheel her out so she could have company. She told me about Pago Pago, where she was from. Sometimes, right as she was talking about living in thatched huts or fishing with nets, she'd fall asleep on the couch, and Mako and I would laugh. She made me call her Matutua, Samoan for grandmother.

Mako and I watched a video — just a regular one, Charles Bronson — and then I crashed on the couch at around two in the morning. Sometime around dawn I woke to the sound of him crying in the bedroom, making a low moan like *O-hoh-hoh*, which I'd heard him do before. I thought it might have to do with his grandma, who'd died the year before, though I'd heard him doing it *before* she died, too, so it could have been anything. I knew that once it started it would go on for a while, though, so I got up and wrote a note that said, *Thanks for everything, Mak, I'll call you from Phoenix*, and left it on the coffee table. Then I crept out of the house and got back on the highway.

The air was cool and the sky was black until I hit Tumacacori, and then the sunrise was one of those ones you don't want to see because you haven't slept enough and are feeling on edge. My hands were shaking. I didn't want to shoot up, because I had a policy against doing it in the morning, but eventually I pulled over and forced myself to smoke a little, just lying down in the car with the seat back as far as it would go. I put a bunch of tapes on, trying to find something mellow, but that was not going to happen, given my tape collection. I thought about something Uncle Philip had said one time: that at a certain point in your life country-western music is the only thing you want to hear. And then I suddenly wanted to go home and listen to country music and be a different kind of guy, an upstanding American kid, though I wasn't even a kid anymore, but a twenty-six-year-old man, which was somehow surprising to me. Fortunately, I was already feeling the heroin by this time, and I got out of the car and walked into the desert for a while, just going through the saguaros until the sun was warm and pressing against me.

When I pulled up to Mullin's he was out in the yard, sitting against the trunk of a palm tree. He had a duffel bag at his feet.

"What the hell?" I said, getting out of the car.

"Thought I might join you," he said. He stood and brushed grass from his jeans.

"You gotta be kidding," I said.

"I'm serious as a heart attack, Boone."

"What about Sandy?"

"I'd a lot rather you didn't mention her name right now. She'll be here any minute with Mark, so we gotta split. We all good?"

"Yeah," I said, but I wasn't good at all. I felt uneasy about him coming, and I didn't like the idea of him leaving Sandy like that. "Let me grab a beer from the fridge," I said, just wanting some time to think about it. He picked up his duffel bag and followed me inside.

"Everything go right in Nogales?" he asked.

"Yeah, sure. What would go wrong?"

"You got the stuff, then?"

"The meth? Yeah, it's in my pocket."

"No, the other," he said, with a shit-eating grin.

"The heroin? Yeah, of course. It's in the car."

"Man, I've been waiting a long time for this," he said, an almost spiritual look on his face. "Ten months, and not a day goes by when I don't think about it."

I was surprised he was so intense about the heroin, since he'd gotten so far away from it. I hadn't imagined he'd get back into it right away. I was also a little annoyed that he couldn't even pretend there were other reasons for coming along, like the company of a guy he'd said was the best friend he'd ever had. I got a beer and opened it, looking out the kitchen window.

"What are you gonna to do with that bike?" I asked. It was standing outside beside a low chain-link fence.

"Leave it here," he said. "Sandy can sell it, get some cash."

"She won't get much," I said.

"Yeah, well, let's go, all right? You can drink that in the car. I'll drive."

I saw the picture of Sandy and the kid on the fridge. "She's really gonna freak when she finds out you're gone," I said.

He cut me a look. "What's the matter with you, Boone? You think I need to hear that now? Don't piss me off, all right?"

I was in a mood to piss him off, though. I took the picture down and tossed it onto the table. "You should take this one with you," I said.

"Why do you want to be an asshole, Boone?"

"I guess I forgot what a sensitive guy you are."

"Look, if you don't want me to come, just say so."

"No, no. It's cool. You can come."

"All right, then, let's go. Jesus." He picked up his duffel bag and went to the door, gazing outside with a tormented look on his face.

"Hey, did I ever tell you my brother Alex has Down's syndrome?" I asked.

"Please don't fuck with me, Boone."

"Why do you think I'm fucking with you? I'm telling you

about my brother," I said. "I don't think I ever told you he had Down's syndrome before."

Mullin looked at me as if I'd gone completely crazy. "Can we talk about this some other time? You understand Sandy's coming home right now, don't you?"

I thought about Sandy leaving the Kalil plant, driving home to drop the kid off. She'd probably miss her test now because there'd be no one home to baby-sit.

"What the hell's gotten into you, Boone?" Mullin said from the doorway.

"I just think you're an asshole," I said. "I think it's weird that you don't seem to realize that."

He shook his head and said, "Un-fucking-believable."

"Say it," I said. "Say, 'I'm an asshole.' Then we'll go."

"Fuck off, Boone."

"Come on, say it. Then we can leave, I promise."

He narrowed his eyes, his jaw clenched tight. "I'm an asshole, all right? Now can we leave already?"

"Say, 'Boone's in charge.' One more thing. Just say that."

"Godammit, Boone! I'm not in the mood for this."

"Just one more thing," I said. "Then we'll go, I swear."

"Boone's in charge," he said, staring at me. "Are you satisfied?"

"I don't know," I said. "I don't think I am, for some reason."

A smile came to his lips, like he might start to laugh, like he was waiting for the punch line. I wasn't about to laugh. I'd never hated anyone so much in my life. I had a sip of beer, holding his gaze, pushing him as far as I thought I could push him. Then I set the can on the counter, picked up the picture of Sandy and the kid, and followed him out to the car.

Crossroads

I'd told my mom I'd be at Charlie Peck's, play-ing with his new ham radio. This was a lie. It was the first day of June, and I was in my brother's Charger, riding west on Guada-lupe Road. Seth and I were on our way to see Led Zeppelin at Sun Devil Stadium, my first concert aside from seeing José Feliciano at the county fair. I was eleven. My brother was eighteen. He drove in his usual manner, a hand draped over the wheel, eyes cast coolly ahead.

As the traffic slowed at Rural Road, we heard music rising out of the cars around us — Chevy vans and Volkswagen Beetles and faux-wood-paneled wagons. Bare-chested guys hung out the win-dows with beers in their hands. A thin, freckled kid in a truck ahead of us kept lighting Black Cats with a cigarette cherry, then flicking them just before they popped. I smelled gunpowder and suntan lotion and exhaust fumes.

"Whole Lotta Love" came on the radio, and I remembered what I'd read in *Guitar Player* magazine: that Jimmy Page had used a steel slide on the song, then overmixed it with a lot of backward echo. I knew a million facts about Led Zeppelin, because I spent afternoons in the periodicals section of the local library reading articles about them.

"They better play this one," I said.

"They'll play it," Seth said, "unless they want a riot on their hands."

Soon the residential streets gave way to lemon groves and fruit stands, and then we were into fields of yellow weeds. The Cudahy–Bar S plant slipped past, and I watched for my father, who worked the day shift there butchering cattle. I'd seen him walking out to his pickup with his work buddies a few times. In the spring, he'd had a full dark beard and mustache, and then, only weeks later, he had the kind of handlebar mustache worn by Catfish Hunter of the Oakland A's. It bothered me that he could change like that, as if he were doing it to confuse me or keep me off his trail. He'd left our mother two years before and lived with a half-Supai woman named Tina Traitor, who sold turquoise jewelry at flea markets. I'd heard he drank a lot, but I got this information from my mother, who wasn't a reliable source.

Seth watched the plant disappear. For a minute it looked as though he might say something about our father. But instead he took an empty root beer can from the footwell and hung a line of tobacco spit into the hole. We weren't close. I knew he'd rather have his girlfriend, Kim, in the car instead of me. She'd broken up with him two weeks before, after he'd gotten together with a girl named Milena Perez at a canal party. Taking me to the concert must have seemed a better way of appearing repentant than going with Harvey or Russell, his juvey-d friends.

Through my smoke-lensed glasses I watched the kids in the other cars—older boys with lean, hungry faces, girls with straight hair and eye shadow. I wore sunglasses in those days because I had an eye condition known as divergent strabismus, which made my eyes point in two slightly different directions. The problem had earned me the nickname Mackerel at school and, along with my timidity, had made me an outcast. I always hoped something would happen to make me look like Seth, who had what my grandmother Henderson called "classic features." People said he looked like Michael Sarrazin, an actor who'd been in movies like *Sometimes a Great Notion* and *They Shoot Horses, Don't They?*

We passed a Nile-green Firebird, inside of which a group of guys were handing a bottle around.

"You ever get drunk, Wren?" Seth asked.

"One time," I said.

"When did you get drunk?" he asked, sounding surprised.

"Well, not drunk, exactly. But Charlie Peck and I ate a rum cake once and ran around the golf course."

"That doesn't get you drunk."

"I could feel it," I insisted.

"You didn't feel it," he said. "We'll pick up a six-pack and I'll teach you to shotgun." He eased a little farther back in his seat.

As we passed the cattle yards, Seth's smile faded. I knew he'd had little to be happy about lately. Aside from his romantic problems and the situation at home, there was a matter so serious I had to put it out of my mind for long periods of time: Seth was going to Southeast Asia. In a fit of frustration over his SAT scores, which were too low for the school Kim would go to, he'd taken a bus downtown and enlisted in the Marine Corps. It had been a big deal around the house, with heated discussions at the dinner table and my Uncle Gus going down to the office of our congressman, Morris Udall. But in the end nothing could be done about it. Seth would go to Camp Pendleton, near San Diego, on August fifth. After twenty-four weeks of boot camp and artillery training, he'd be on his way to Vietnam.

We stopped at a liquor store on Apache — a squat brick place called Johnnie Haze. The aisles were packed with guys in cutoffs and girls in shorts and sandals, all of them gathering food and alcohol for the show. I was getting butterflies in my stomach, the way I did before flag football games. Though I'd listened to Led Zeppelin's records hundreds of times and had posters of the band all over my walls, I couldn't help feeling as if I was too young for the concert. I was sure I'd glance up and see my mom at the end of the snack aisle or turn around to find that Seth had left me.

At the beverage coolers, I suggested we get the sixteen-ounce Budweisers our dad always drank. Seth shook his head at this and slid a six-pack of Hamm's off the rack. "You don't shotgun a tall-boy," he said.

As we waited in line, I watched the clerk, a heavy-set Mexican with a braided ponytail. In a low, rumbling voice he kept asking customers if they were on their way to the concert. If they said yes he'd give them a pained look and say, "You're killing me, you know that?" I couldn't tell whether he was serious or not.

When it was our turn, he gave me a hard look that made me glad I'd kept my glasses on.

"You look smart, kid," he said. "Think you can tell me why I'm stuck here tonight?"

"Maybe you did something wrong," I suggested. I knew Seth liked it when I played the smart aleck. "Maybe you're being punished."

"You think God's trying to put the screws to me, huh?"

"Could be."

"That would be just like him." He winked at my brother. "You guys going to the concert?"

"Yeah," Seth said.

"Lucky dogs," he said, and slid our beers into a bag.

Walking out to the gravel lot, Seth said, "You've gotten to be a regular wiseass, Wren. It's impressive."

I felt the tips of my ears go warm, as they always did when I was embarrassed. Seth's car was at the edge of the lot, the sun low and red behind it. The sky was all shot through with ribbons of orange and gold. Before getting into the Charger, I did something I'd never done before: I took a small gray pebble from the blacktop, rubbed it on my shirttail, and set it on my tongue like a vitamin pill. After working up some spit, I swallowed it.

"What the hell, Wren?" Seth said, looking at me sideways.

"To commemorate the occasion," I said. "You should do it, too."

He laughed and shook his head, but I knew he'd do it. In a good mood you could get him to do a lot of things. He set the beer on the car hood and looked for a good-sized pebble, then put it on his tongue and swallowed it just as I had.

"Happy?" he asked.

"Yeah," I said. "This way we'll never forget what happened."

And I was right.

We pulled into the parking lot as a helicopter settled over the far end of the stadium, its blades cutting the air with a *thut-thut* sound I felt in my collarbone. It was a Lockheed 286, I happened to know, because I'd done a report on helicopters for social studies. I knew it was on its way to the med center, transporting a trauma victim from one of the nearby highways. Seth watched it with a solemnity that made me sure he was thinking of the helicopters we saw on the nightly news, marine Hueys that pulled dead soldiers out of the jungle.

"That's them, Wren," he said, and glanced at me. "The Zeppelin has landed."

"You think that's the band?" I'd clearly seen the red cross on the bottom of the chopper.

"What do you think, they take a cab from the hotel?"

He pulled a beer out of the bag, then dug into his front pocket for the jackknife my dad had given him. A rush of dizziness came over me when I saw the knife. I loved its pearly sheen and the surprising weight of it when you held it in your hand.

"All right," Seth said. "Observe."

He cut a pea-sized hole near the bottom of the can, covered the hole with a thumb, then turned the can upright and pressed the hole to his lips. After popping the tab, he swallowed as fast as he could, and his Adam's apple jumped up and down. He seemed in pain until he was able to belch, and then he grinned at me.

"Think you can handle that?"

I watched him carefully as he cut the hole. He brought the can to my mouth, popped the tab, and the beer rushed down my throat. I thought of my pebble sloshing around in my stomach.

"Not bad for a little cactus wren," Seth said.

"I think I feel it," I told him.

He laughed. "You'll feel it when you get out of the car."

"Why's that?"

"Way it is," he said.

It was seven-twenty, according to my Timex Twist-o-Flex. The show was to begin at eight o'clock. Wild-looking hippies in kaftans and beads streamed past us, followed by groups of girls in tight iron-on T-shirts. I saw a guy who looked the way I hoped to look when I was his age — thin, inconspicuously handsome. Across from us, a band of guys were playing acoustic guitars in the back of a pickup. People danced. The smell of pot smoke came through the windows. Seth leaned forward and punched the cigarette lighter, then took one of his Tiparillos out of a pack on the dash.

"Wonder what Kim's up to," he said.

"Probably sitting at home, wishing she were here," I said, because I wanted him to feel good about her.

He nodded, but I didn't think I'd convinced him. I was sure Seth and Kim would get back together, because she was crazy about him. Of all the girls Seth had gone with, Kim was my favorite — a smart, pretty girl who played tenor saxophone and wanted to be a veterinarian, which was what I had always wanted to be.

"You know, I'm thinking about buying her a ring," Seth said.

"That's a good idea. Girls always like jewelry."

He smiled, his mouth slightly open as if he were about to laugh. It took me a minute to understand what he was getting at.

"A *wedding* ring?" I asked.

He burst out laughing. "Well, an engagement ring," he said. "Though you gotta buy both, I guess. The engagement ring's the one with the diamond."

"Holy shit!"

"I know," he said, nodding, and then a serious mood seemed to take him. He brought a beer from the bag and opened it in the regular way. "I'm really thinking about it, Wren. I swear to God."

"You should," I said. "You really should."

I felt almost as if I were going to marry Kim myself. I could see her gold-flecked eyes, the smile that brought a dimple high on her cheek. I felt an odd sense of relief, too, because it seemed that if Seth married Kim he'd have to make it home from Asia, though of course there was no logical reason to think so. I thought of how happy our mom would be. And then I remembered the lie I'd told her and was suddenly worried.

"I shouldn't have told her I was at Peck's," I said, my voice high pitched and childish sounding.

"Who?" Seth said. "What are you talking about?"

"Mom," I said. "What if she calls there?"

"Why would she call Peck's?"

I couldn't think of any reason. I pictured our mom on the couch at home, assembling the missionary medical kits she made for the church, rolling three-foot strips of gauze into bundles. Just out the window, a skinny man writhed to the sound of someone's car stereo, his hair hanging around him like a curtain, his feet bare and dirty.

"She wouldn't have let you come if you'd told the truth," Seth said.

"I know it."

"There's no telling what she'll do these days," he said.

For several months, our mom had belonged to a church called East Phoenix Pentecostal, and we'd watched her change from the wry, dispirited woman she'd been to a kind of beatific stranger. She wore long skirts instead of jeans, and she no longer drank Chablis. She prayed each night, as part of the contract she'd made with other church members, who called every day or so to see how she was doing. She smiled in a strange, otherworldly way.

"She never even jokes around anymore," I said. "She used to joke around all the time."

"She's changed, Wren," Seth said. "There's nothing you can do about it."

"I almost feel like I don't like her anymore," I said.

"Don't say that. You like her."

"I know," I said.

"She doesn't have to know everything you do, though. You're eleven now. When I was eleven I was sneaking out of the house and everything. Kip and I stole that sewing machine when we were only ten."

"I know."

"We did all kinds of things," he said.

I didn't want to do the things Seth had done, though — running around with degenerates, stealing things they didn't even want. I'd gotten an acoustic guitar for Christmas, and what I wanted to do was learn to play it well enough to form a band once I got to high school. That was my plan. I wasn't good looking like Seth, and I knew I never would be, but I was smarter than he was and willing to work hard, and there seemed the slimmest chance that these qualities might be important, too.

Seth was right about the beer, though. As I stepped out of the car I felt an explosion of warmth in my head, and it was suddenly a pleasure just to be inside my body. I felt loose limbed and full of good cheer, like the Scarecrow in *The Wizard of Oz*.

"I could get used to this," I said.

"Okay, cowboy," said Seth.

We walked across the scorching parking lot, past rows of vans and dirty-faced hippies, people selling trinkets from the backs of pickups. After waiting in a long, slow line, we handed over our tickets to a bored-looking security guard; then it was up into the concrete stadium, where the air was cool and dry. A glimpse of the crowd through the section gate took my breath away. Here were eighty thousand people filling the high stadium walls, milling around like insects on the field. The opposite rim of the bowl could have been a mile away, it looked so small and grainy through the smoke-filled air. I saw the stage near the southern end zone, black and spare, two huge walls of speakers rising on either side. John Bonham's pearl drum kit sparkled in the dim light. Jimmy Page's guitars stood in a line near the front. I tried to tell which was the Gibson, which was the Strat, but they were too far away. Slowly, I became aware of the sound of the crowd, a low sea sound, like a shell pressed to my ear.

"Jesus, Wren," Seth said. "They could have sold out ten nights in a row here, I bet. That must be like being a king or something."

"They could probably be president," I said, "even though they're not even Americans."

"You're wasted," he said.

"I am not," I said, but I was feeling no pain.

We walked down to the field, eighty-seven concrete steps. The grass was springy for football season. People around us were strangely subdued, as if pausing to turn inside themselves before the show began. Burly guys with biker mustaches looked almost in prayer as they stared at the band risers. An enormous beach ball was going around, but the crowd was too distracted to keep it up for long.

"If we get separated," Seth said, "meet me by that Texaco sign." He pointed at a red sign beneath the announcer's booth, then saw the fear in my eyes and added, "I'm saying just in case."

We found a place on the left side of the soundboard, thirty or so yards from the stage. Blankets lay scattered on the grass, but everyone was standing. I was fascinated by the soundboard and by the long-haired technicians who stood over the controls, talking to one another in British accents. People around us smoked pot and glanced at the stage. Seth opened a beer he'd smuggled in and we passed it back and forth.

"It's a strange world," he said, gazing off at the stadium wall. "It's weird to think anything bad could be going on anywhere else, you know?"

"Yeah, I know," I said.

"I could handle just hanging out in a scene like this for the next few years. Going to concerts, having a blast."

"No shit," I said.

I tried to think of something else to say, because I knew he was thinking about the war, and I was sure we wouldn't get this close to talking about it again before he left. But there was nothing in my life that offered any insight into what he faced.

"People call me Mackerel at school," I finally said—I didn't know why. I'd just been thinking about it, about how the nickname made people notice what I hated most about myself. I thought about it all the time.

"Who calls you that?" Seth said, narrowing his eyes.

"Oh, nobody," I said, "just everyone at school."

"Charlie Peck doesn't, does he?"

"Not Charlie," I said. "Just some of the guys."

"That's bullshit," he said, peering at me as if I were one of the name-callers myself. I saw a line of whiskers he'd missed along his jaw line when he shaved that morning. "People say I look like Michael Sarrazin," he said, and frowned as if it bothered him, though I knew it didn't. He was proud of the resemblance. The beach ball came our way, and he reached up and punched it with his fist, and that seemed to end the conversation. At least he was no longer worrying about the war, I thought.

Eight o'clock came and went, then eight-thirty and nine. The air was thick with what the television commercials called "nervous perspiration." Waves of shouting rose and died away. Finally, at twenty to ten, the stadium lights cut out and the crowd erupted into the loudest screams I'd ever heard.

"Here we go!" Seth yelled, his voice barely audible over the roar.

The band took the stage, ghostly figures in the dark. The first thing out of the amplifiers was the intro to "Rock and Roll," and its heavy snare drums were like a fist against my chest. Robert Plant strolled into a beam of white light, tossing his hair back, singing, "Been a long time since I rock and rolled!" John Paul Jones was there in his pageboy, laying down the bass. And then I saw Jimmy Page, a thin man dressed all in black.

We'd heard the rumors about Led Zeppelin, that they were into devil worship and had sold their souls, that they'd bought the old manor of Aleister Crowley and conducted occult rituals there. Watching Jimmy Page, I knew it was all true. He had moons and pentagrams stitched down his pant legs, and the sound that came out of his amplifiers seemed straight from the core of the earth. It was more than the music and the clothes though, more than the cool way he hopped and swayed. Jimmy was not handsome, not like my brother; he was thin and pale and unusual looking, like me. And yet he was the coolest man I'd ever seen. You could imagine him as a skinny kid in England, with acne scars and glasses, even divergent strabismus.

He played it soft on "Since I Been Loving You," bending the strings, working the vibrato. I wanted to get closer and watch his fingers on the frets, see him do the tricks I'd read about in *Guitar Player* and *Creem*.

I turned to Seth to ask if he'd cut through the crowd with me, but he was talking to a skinny blond girl in a crocheted sundress. She had dark eyes, set wide apart, and was holding a big jug of wine in her hands like a pumpkin. She laughed at something Seth said. I could see her nipples through the fabric of her dress.

"See something you like?" she asked me, her eyes filled with playful accusation.

"Not really," I said.

"That's Wayne," Seth said, laughing. "He's the cactus wren."

"He likes to look at the ladies," she said, and stared at me. There was an air of recklessness about her, which might have come from the few inches of wine she'd already drunk. She held out the jug and said, "Want some?"

"No thanks," I said.

"He's already drunk," Seth said.

"I am not," I said, but I was.

"How about a kiss, then?" she said. She set the jug on the grass and came to me, smelling of wine and sandalwood and something deeper, something dark and mysterious. She was older than I'd imagined, twenty-five or -six, with a gap between her front teeth and sharp lines at the corners of her eyes. She took my face in her hands and kissed me on the mouth, then went back to Seth and kissed him in a different way, her whole body pressed against his, her hips rolling. She was exciting and vulgar, and I was impressed that Seth had been able to find her so quickly, though it worried me that he could forget all about Kim, whom he'd just told me he wanted to marry.

The band was finishing up "Since I Been Loving You," thundering their way through the heavy, tragic out-section. They pressed towels to their faces and gazed out over the crowd. Jimmy strapped on a Les Paul and launched into "Whole Lotta Love," the song I'd been waiting for. The opening riff was even heavier than on the album. Robert Plant came in with the wailing vocal.

I kept looking back at Seth and the woman, though. At one point she held his hand like a palm reader, telling him what she saw. Later she was doing a dance for him in an island style. Seth watched with a joint in his mouth, a proprietary grin on his face. He reminded me of our dad in some of the old photos I'd seen.

On stage, Jimmy drifted into "Ten Years Gone," playing the twelve-string neck of his double-neck Gibson; then he switched to the six string and really rocked. "Dazed and Confused" was next, with Plant howling the blues, then John Bonham's drum solo, "Moby Dick." I don't think any of us in the crowd had thought the band would work this hard for us, not in our embarrassing little city in the middle of desert. With Bonzo leaning into the drum kit, smacking the skins with his bare hands, I was overcome with a feeling of gratitude, as if the effort itself were making my life more valid, more real.

By the end of the set my brother and the woman lay spread out on rumpled blankets, touching each other in a dreamy, experimental way. I called Seth's name, but he didn't turn around, so I waded into the crowd on my own. It was easier to get close than I'd expected. Huge tattooed guys let me walk right past them. I joined the conversation of three guys from Philadelphia, who were arguing about which encore song the band would play first. Two said "Stairway to Heaven," while the other voted for "Communication Breakdown." I said, "'Black Dog', no question," and they all cracked up at my bravado.

I ended up half a dozen yards from the stage, where the air was hotter than it had been at the soundboards. The crowd was tight. A sudden undulation knocked me forward, and my glasses fell to the ground. I had no way of bending over to get them, though I could feel them through the thin soles of my Keds. No one seemed to notice. People were talking and laughing, and I was where I'd wanted to be, smelling the electricity coming off the amplifiers. Then the band returned, and the crowd got so tight my feet rose briefly from the ground.

Robert Plant sang, "Hey, hey, mamma, said the way you move, gonna make you sweat, gonna make you groove!" It was the opening of "Black Dog," and I turned and shouted, "I was right!" but the Philadelphia guys were long gone now. The sound up front was so loud I could feel the wind of it on my face. I watched Jimmy make his tricky chord progressions, playing a deep-red Fender, the most beautiful guitar I'd ever seen.

As he strapped his guitar on for the next song, his eyes brushed the front of the crowd, and for a moment I was sure they settled on my own. I might have imagined it — Jimmy's pale face, a flash of recognition — but, for the effect the moment had on me, he might as well have mouthed the words "Follow me." I knew just as surely as I knew anything that I would be a guitarist in a rock band and play the big stadiums of the world, pressing the deep parts of myself into the guitar, hearing them rise out of the amplifiers. It wasn't until much later that I remembered I'd lost my glasses, and then it seemed possible that Jimmy had noticed me only because I looked unusual, because there was something wrong with my eyes.

I was hardly aware of the next two songs. One of them, "Stairway," worked the crowd into a frenzy. The other may have been "The Lemon Song" or "Boogie with Stu," one of their blues send-ups. Finally, the lights flashed on, and the band left the stage. I was a little shell-shocked — my ears ringing, my body drenched with sweat. It took a while for people to ease back from the proscenium, and by the time they did I was so used to being propped up I could hardly stand on my own. I made my way through the litter-strewn stadium, passing bottles and cans, fried chicken containers. Near the soundboards, I saw one of the guys from Philadelphia, and he raised a fist at me. "Yo, Black Dog!" he shouted. "Rock on, man!"

Back at the car, Seth had the blond woman up against the passenger door. They were making out, running their hands over each other's body. She saw me first but didn't seem to know who I was, so she punched Seth's arm to make him turn around.

"Wren!" he said, his face lighting up. "What did you think of the show, buddy?"

"Oh, man!" I said.

"This is Alma," he said. "We're giving her a ride home."

She squinted at me, leaning forward. "Did something happen to your eye?"

It was only then that I remembered my sunglasses. I felt the tips of my ears go warm.

"It's just something he always had," Seth told her. "It's no big deal."

"I thought he got poked with a stick or something," she said, and gave a nervous laugh.

I didn't like her after that. Under the bright parking lot lights, she looked older and less pretty than before. For a frightening moment, I thought she might be as old as our mom, but she wasn't nearly that old — just a woman who'd been in the world long enough for it to show on her face. She had spilled wine all down the front of her dress. I thought she was pathetic.

I climbed into the backseat and tried to hold on to the feeling I'd had at the show. I didn't want to lose any of that because of Alma. As we merged into a long line of cars, I looked at the girls in other cars, younger girls who didn't seem as frightening as they had before the show. I was thinking that if I worked hard enough at playing guitar I might be able to have any of them I wanted. Looking at them in such a hopeful state, it was as if they were already mine.

On the way to Alma's, Seth hummed "No Quarter" and smoked one of her Virginia Slims. We were taking Indian School Road past wide-open fields of yucca and chaparral. I felt the hum of the muffler under my thighs. An oil refinery stood off the side of the road, its red lights flashing. Beyond it were a few small houses and unmarked crossways. Alma told Seth to make a left at one of these, and we drove until we came to a small blue house set off in a sloping field of weeds. A floodlamp lit the front yard. All the windows were dark.

Alma had been leaning into Seth the whole way home, kissing his ear, sliding a hand under his T-shirt. Now, with the car parked, she climbed onto his lap and kissed him full on the mouth, pulling his face toward her like he was something to drink. The sound of their mouths disgusted me. I sat looking at the moon, thinking about my mother, who would probably be in bed by now, reading her Bible or the Book of Psalms. I was somehow sure she'd be thinking of me. After a few minutes, Seth turned and said, "I'm gonna go in for a while."

"Why?" I asked, but he only laughed and got out of the car.

I watched them walk down the bank of weeds. Alma had the jug in her hands, just a few inches of wine at the bottom now. A light came on in the living room, and I watched them kissing in there, then watched Seth take Alma's crocheted dress by the hem and lift it off in one motion. She wore light blue panties. Her skin was dark except for the pale line around her breasts, which were small. Seth kissed her for a moment, then led her down the hall. I knew I could walk down the slope and watch them — there were no blinds on any of the windows — but I'd already seen all I wanted to see.

I got out and walked down Indian School Road, humming "The Wanton Song" in the dark, smelling the sage that grew all around me. An enormous chinaberry tree stood in a field near a crossroads, and I threw rocks at it until I could hit it every time. I had read in a magazine that the bluesman Robert Johnson sold his soul to the devil by standing at a crossroads on a night like this, waiting for the beast to come along and fine-tune his guitar. It made me nervous; it seemed such an easy thing to do, like putting your hand on a Bible or swallowing a stone, something you could almost do by accident. I wondered if Page and the rest of the band had stood at a crossroads like that, and I wondered what it would be like once you'd sold your soul — whether you'd have to think about it every day or could just forget about it for weeks at a time and enjoy your fame. The whole thing scared me, but in the back of my mind I toyed with the possibility of trying it someday.

As I walked back to Alma's, I heard something move through the sage and was suddenly afraid, thinking the devil had over-heard my thoughts. I started spitting out the Lord's Prayer: "Our Father, who art in Heaven. . . ." But then a jackrabbit shot out from behind a sage bush and my heart stopped pounding. I went back to the car and listened to people calling into KUPD. They were speaking about the concert in reverent tones that seemed to justify all the things I'd felt. Dusty James, my favorite DJ, played "Communication Breakdown," then came back saying, "Were you there, baby? Did you make it to the biggest thing to ever hit the valley of the sun?"

"I was there," I said to the dashboard. "You're damn right I was."

Seth came out of the house half an hour later, tucking his shirt in, letting the screen door slap shut behind him. He jogged halfway up the slope, then broke into a sprint, grinning at me through the windshield. I smelled Alma's perfume as he slid into the seat beside me.

"She's married!" he said, gazing down at the little house. "Her husband's in Tucson, but they've got a kid and everything!"

I couldn't understand why any of this would excite him. "How old *is* she?" I asked.

"Twenty-six," he said, and gave me a serious look. "That's older than some of my teachers, Wren."

"Where's the kid at?"

"You think I asked her about that?" He laughed as he slid the key into the ignition, and the Charger roared to life. Our headlights struck the pale blue side of the building.

We had to dip into Alma's yard to turn around, which brought us close to the big front window. As we passed, I saw Alma come into the room with no clothes on at all, hands on her hips, a cigarette dangling from her mouth. I saw the dark triangle between her legs. She seemed to notice our car in the yard and came to the window, and then she did something I'll never forget: As if to cool herself, she leaned against the glass, her breasts flattening to white circles, her nipples dark in the center. She kissed the window and smiled out at us in a sleepy, intoxicated way.

"Jesus," Seth said, "are you seeing this?"

"What the hell's she doing that for?"

He hit the gas, and we fishtailed through the weeds and bumped onto the road with a jolt that shook me against the door. Seth was laughing, cranking the wheel with both hands to get us going straight. As he pulled away, I glanced back through the dust and saw the house, but Alma was no longer at the window.

"Sometimes they just go crazy," he said, shaking his head, grinning. "It's a good feeling, actually. Makes you feel powerful." He leaned back and thought for a while, his head cocked up as if he were listening for a noise. "Man, I feel like something big is going to happen to me. You ever get that feeling?"

"Everybody gets that," I said.

"I got it now pretty bad," he said, looking out the windshield. "I got it pretty serious right now."

We passed the oil refinery with its flashing lights. I saw two men up on the platform wearing construction hats that shone in the dark.

"So what do you think will happen?" I asked.

"Something big," he said. "Something exciting." He widened his eyes.

"You're going to Vietnam," I said.

Seth cut his eyes at me. "Jesus, Wayne, what's the matter with you?"

"Nothing," I said, but I knew I shouldn't have mentioned the war.

"You don't even know what I'm talking about," he said, glancing out at the desert. "Just forget about it."

I did know what he was talking about, though — or I thought I did. Seth had been affected by the night in the same way I had, and now he was feeling the sense of possibility that had opened up before him. If I'd tried to shut him down, it was only because we were such different people. I didn't see how we could both get what we wanted.

"I'll go to the war," he said, looking me hard in the eye, "but I'll come back and do whatever I want to do. You hear me? I'll go places and see whatever I want to see."

"All right," I said. "I know you will."

"People will know who I am," he said.

We were easing past the dismantling yards. The smell of creosote came through the windows.

"What do you think you'll do?" I asked, because I wanted him to know I believed him.

"Who cares? Make lots of money. Be an actor, be a singer. Be in a band."

"What about Kim? You think you'll marry her still?"

He laughed as if it were a half-baked idea I'd come up with on my own. "Who knows?" he said. "I love Kim, but she's small time, you know? She could live and die right here in Arizona and it wouldn't bother her a bit."

"I like her," I said.

"I know *you* like her," he said. "That's exactly what I'm talking about."

"What do you mean?"

"Forget it," he said. "There are things you can't understand until you're older. Maybe not even then. Your life is gonna be different than mine."

"I bet it will be," I said.

We were both happy to think so.

There were no other cars on the road, so Seth pushed the Charger to eighty-five and ninety miles an hour, swerving from shoulder to shoulder, making the car lean into its struts. He laughed and stared out at the road as if his future lay just ahead. I told him to slow down, but it only made him go faster, and then the road made a sharp turn to the right and he nearly lost control of the car. He slowed down after that, hunched over the wheel, a sheepish grin on his face. He was stoned and a little drunk, but when he was straight he wasn't much smarter. I can't say I ever thought he'd make it home from Vietnam.

He did make it home, though, nineteen months later, on a hot Tuesday afternoon in March. I had skipped class that day to walk along the canal banks near Papago Park, something I did from time to time. I hated middle school. I'd lost touch with the few elementary school buddies I'd had, including my best friend, Charlie Peck. I spent most of my time bent over a cheap electric guitar in my bedroom, trying to copy guitar leads from the records I liked. I almost never got them right. There were small improvements — I knew the chords and could keep a rhythm — but I had nothing you might consider God-given talent. The more I learned about the guitar, the more I realized this was going to be a problem.

My mom had been in and out of the hospital by this time. She'd been diagnosed with borderline personality disorder and put on a drug called Mellaril, which made her sleep too much and caused her to gain weight. She lost her job as a receptionist but got one as church secretary for the Pentecostals, who paid her just enough to get by. She was pious and dull-eyed and hard to be with. I avoided her as much as possible.

I saw Kim now and then. She was studying veterinary medicine at Arizona State, and she also taught music two days a week at the high school. She'd smile when she saw me and ask me about my guitar playing. She was one of the few people who ever seemed happy to see me.

When I got home that day in March, a metal trunk lay on the front stoop. Seth's name and rank were stenciled across the top — S. E. Clayton, Private Second Class. At first I thought he must have been killed, because he hadn't written to say he was coming home, though this was the time when people were coming home, the end of the war, the months before the fall of Saigon. My mother was crying on the sofa when I went inside, buckled over as if someone had punched her in the stomach.

"What happened?" I asked.

She glanced up, her eyes filled with wonder. "God sent him home," she said.

Seth was in his room, taking clothes out of a duffel bag, putting them into his dresser drawers. He looked taller than I'd remembered, his shoulders broader, his neck thick and brown. He wore his hair in a regulation high-and-tight and had grown a mustache. He no longer looked like Michael Sarrazin or anyone else I could think of. Something in his manner kept me from hugging him or even shaking his hand.

"So what's the program, Wayne?" he asked, nodding at me in a casual way, as if we'd just spoken a few minutes ago. I noticed that his hands were trembling. He squeezed them and slid them into his pockets.

"When did you get back?" I asked.

"About an hour ago." He put a khaki shirt into a dresser drawer, glancing out the window. He seemed to be on the alert for something in the yard. "So what's the story with Mom?" he asked. "She seems pretty messed up."

"How do you mean?"

"She won't stop crying."

From the living room came a low moan. "She's been praying since you left," I said. "I guess she's happy."

"I guess," he said, and went back to his unpacking, his posture stiff and precise. After a moment, feeling dismissed, I left the room.

He was quiet at dinner. My mother and I asked him questions, which he answered briefly, staring at his plate of fish sticks and corn. He told us he'd been stationed in a town called My Tho, near the Mekong River delta. He'd spent most of his days in a seven-foot artillery trench, guarding a bridge, but had seen very little action. He spoke as if briefing other soldiers. I didn't ask him what I wanted to know—whether he had killed a man, whether he had seen anyone get killed.

He stayed in his room the next couple of days, listening to the radio, watching the small black-and-white television on his dresser. He took long showers and slept a lot. Half a dozen times I tried to have a conversation with him, but I never got far. He'd put me off with vague looks or say he was tired. I gave up asking him to look at my new guitar. Once I turned my amp up loud, so he'd hear me down the hall, but he never said anything about my playing.

On his first Friday night back, he went out and didn't come home until three in the morning, then packed a duffel bag in his bedroom and left again. From my bedroom window, I watched him walk out to the Charger and put the bag in the trunk. He got in, lit a cigarette, and looked up at the house. He could have been leaving for a couple of days, but somehow I knew it would be longer than that. Later I learned that he'd seen Kim that night, but she never told me what happened between them.

I went into his bedroom, where his trunk lay open on the bed. I took out some clothes and medals and a bottle of Jameson's whisky wrapped in an olive T-shirt. Farther down there was a stack of letters, mostly from Kim and my mom. One was from me, a half-page note in which I described my new guitar and made no reference at all to the fact that Seth was fighting in a war. I found my father's old jackknife and a lot of eight-track tapes — the Stones and the Who and our old favorite, Led Zeppelin. They rattled when I shook them, because inside was the loamy, black soil of Vietnam. I emptied them out on the bedspread, breathing in the smell of roots. For years afterward, I'd take the tapes out and listen to them, wondering how they made Seth feel when he was in his gunner's trench, when he had no idea whether he'd make it home or if there even was such a place anymore.

Five years later, John Bonham died of alcohol poisoning in Jimmy Page's manor in Windsor. I found out about it in Mr. Armstrong's chemistry class. A group of stoner kids I didn't know were discussing it over a lab table, staring off at the middle distance, shaking their heads. They seemed to take a perverse pleasure in the news, which made me hate them, though I imagine that if I'd been able to share it with them I might have found pleasure in it, too. As it was, I was devastated. I walked out of the classroom, not even bothering to turn as Mr. Armstrong barked my name three times in a row.

I'd become even more of an outcast by then. I'd go to classes but would eat my lunch alone in the empty band room. The year before, I'd had surgery to correct my divergent strabismus, but I couldn't shake my habit of avoiding eye contact. I smoked pot every day anyway, so my eyes were always bloodshot. I still wore sunglasses most of the time.

Late on the night of John Bonham's death, I drove my mom's car out Indian School Road, watching the low houses slip past one by one. It was a warm night, and the smell of swimming pools and orange blossoms came through my windows. There were houses as far out as Goodyear now and a country club where the dismantling yards had been. Once you passed the oil refinery, though, things looked much as they had years before—flat red earth and yuccas, the glowing eyes of jackrabbits on the side of the road.

I'd taken Seth's bottle of Jameson's and was sipping from it as I drove. It made the skin around my eyes pull tight. I'd meant to save the whisky until Seth came back, but I didn't think that would happen now. We'd called all his friends and talked to the police and had stapled copies of his graduation photo to telephone poles all over town. We never heard anything. A few times I thought I saw Seth in a passing car or in a restaurant, but it always turned out to be someone who looked like him, tall, dark haired, and handsome. Once I thought I saw his face on the screen of the Tonelea Drive-In, and I thought, *He made it,* not so much surprised as devastated, because I'd given up on fame by then except in my fantasies. It wasn't Seth on the screen, of course. It was Michael Sarrazin.

I took a left at Alma's road and drove past the old blue house, abandoned and dark now, sitting in weeds up to its window sashes. At a crossroad marked Rural Road West, I parked on the shoulder and took a long sip of the Jameson's. I was thinking of John Bonham, of the way he'd played "Moby Dick" in Sun Devil Stadium so many years before, and of the certainty I'd felt that I'd make it as a lead guitarist. Stepping out of the car, a thought came to me, and I walked to the side of the road and said out loud, *Satan, I relinquish my soul.* Even as I said it, I knew it was ridiculous. The night held not the faintest trace of possibility. There was only the invisible desert all around me and the dull glow of Phoenix over a brace of hills. I stumbled into an empty field and threw up on a bush, more out of a sense of loss than anything.

Afterward, I drove back down the washboard road to Alma's house, where I pulled over and staggered down the slope, drunk in a dull, medicated way. A car battery lay in the weeds near the door, and without thinking I lifted it up and heaved it through the front window. The pane fell away with a ringing sound. I kicked a few toothy shards from the sill and climbed into the room, calling out, "Hey," breathing in the dusty air. The front of the house was mostly empty, but in a back room I found a rocking chair and an unmade bed, and as a kind of game I tried to convince myself that Seth had been living here since I'd seen him last. I went back to the living room, wanting to see him come through the door, wanting to tell him what had happened to my life. I wanted to blame him because things had gotten so much worse for me after he left. But they were bad before he left, too, and it had less to do with him than with other factors. At some point I'd simply become uninterested in the world around me. It was the reason I'd offered to sell my soul in the desert: I needed people to know they'd been wrong about me, needed them to see my face on a magazine and say, *Mackerel's hit the big time.* Anything short of this was like nothing at all — or worse than nothing at all. I was eighteen, and like most eighteen-year-olds I believed in the Neil Young line, "It's better to burn out than to fade away." I couldn't imagine my mind would ever change.

It's painful to think of it now — like watching a movie in which the characters go in all the wrong directions; I sit cringing, wanting to shout instructions to myself. I'm thirty-nine now, and I like to think I have neither burned out nor faded away but instead have found a kind of calm I never anticipated in my life.

That night at Alma's house I walked into the kitchen and broke a few mismatched dishes that lay on the counter. Who knows why? After a while, the sound of the distant highway called me to the window. As I looked out at the dull lights in the distance, I thought of Seth standing in a place like this — a field or a seedy motel room or a truck stop parking lot — and wondered if he was carrying me inside him in some way. Maybe he was at the bottom of his own life then, feeling the approach of a different kind of possibility, the possibility of survival only, of ordinary acceptance. I can't say if it was true. All I know is what happened next: I climbed out the window, went up the slope, and got into the car. In the rearview mirror, Alma's house became smaller as I pulled away from the shoulder; then it disappeared behind a rise in the land. Ahead was the glow of Phoenix. It changed as I approached, growing wider and higher until finally, and without my even noticing, I became a part of it.

Sarah
at the
Palace

Harlan is in Las Vegas, in the dining room of his dead sister's condominium. Through a Mylar-coated window he can see the Strip in the distance, tall and sun stricken above a wall that surrounds the condominium complex. He sees the Luxor, Excalibur, the futuristic spire of the Stratosphere. The city, which once held the power to thrill him, now seems garish and bleak. He looks at it only to escape the condo, which is even bleaker.

It has been six years since he visited, and everything in the condo seems intended to remind him of that fact. In the dining room, hundreds of Styrofoam cups cover the avocado carpet, all in clusters of three. Most have numbers on the inside rim, written in Sarah's nervous hand — 207, 64, 5078. Harlan has no idea what the numbers mean. In the living room, she stacked four-gallon ice-cream tubs into low walls, dividing the room into smaller rooms, giving the place the look of an excavated Mayan village. Aluminum foil has been taped neat as wallpaper over most of the walls and windows, casting the room in an eerie, reflective glow, like a laboratory in an old mad-scientist movie. Dead plants hang over the rims of their pots. Dozens of cats dart in and out of the rooms.

His ex-wife, Marlene, moves between the rows of ice-cream tubs with the careful stride of an archaeologist. They have been divorced five months, and she has recently begun a new life in Tempe — working as a paralegal, seeing a lawyer named Ron. But she agreed to fly from Phoenix with Harlan to help settle Sarah's estate, and he is grateful. She was always good with Sarah, even near the end, when Harlan could hardly bear to talk to his sister on the phone.

Sarah went crazy — that's how the thought keeps coming to him now, as he sorts through the cluttered evidence of her insanity. As a girl she was eccentric, wearing vintage movie-star dresses when everyone else wore tie-dye; in her twenties, when she moved to Vegas and worked as a waitress and part-time showgirl, her life seemed unimaginable to Harlan, though he knew it was the life she wanted. It wasn't until the last few years that she began to unravel, and because Harlan was unraveling too at that time, he did little to help her. Marlene became more like a sibling to Sarah than he'd ever been.

He watches Marlene pick her way across the living room, her melon-colored shirt untucked, her upper lip damp with sweat. She looks prettier than she has in years, thinner and more fit, with a stylish new haircut that softens her features. She leans over a kind of makeshift desk, which Sarah assembled out of several overturned ice-cream tubs. On it are a princess phone and a stack of papers.

"This must be where she talked on the phone," she says, and glances at Harlan gravely. "God, I sure didn't picture the place like this when we talked."

"Me neither," he says.

"You remember coming here after we were married? The place so neat and modern? She had that white furniture and the mirrors everywhere?"

"She used to be neat," he says, remembering his sister's bedroom in their childhood home — the dresses hung according to color and style, her vanity table as precise as a surgeon's tray. He remembers Sarah coming downstairs in a cloud of Jean Naté and the way her appearance silenced the Maricopa High boys who waited, slick, lanky boys who seemed like men to Harlan. He was proud of the effect his sister had on those older boys.

"I wish I'd known how bad it was," he says, frowning.

"How could you know?"

"I should have come," he says.

She sighs. She had urged him to come — many times. She had even offered to come herself. But he'd said no, he'd do it eventually.

Now he glances into Sarah's bedroom, where the vanity table is piled high with stacks of old fashion magazines. On the walls are construction-paper signs with motivational sayings, things like "HANG IN THERE KIDDO!!" and "POWER TO ME!" Near the window is the place where her body was found. Harlan still can't believe it in any sustainable way. It defies prolonged acceptance. Even harder to believe is what the police told him this morning: on the day after Sarah's death, while her body still lay naked on the floor, a group of boys broke a window and came inside. They poked around for an hour or so, judging from the cigarette butts left behind. A neighbor woman who saw them dash out the front door called 911, and that was how the body was discovered. The police didn't think the boys had taken anything or done any harm, but Harlan can't stop thinking about it — strange boys moving through his sister's cluttered condominium, seeing her naked and vulnerable and dead.

"All these tubs have things inside," Marlene is saying behind him.

He turns and watches her pry the lid off an ice-cream tub. Inside it is a Folger's coffee can. Inside the can is a baby-food jar stuffed with tissue.

"They're little mysteries, see?" She unfolds the tissue, and a blue ten-dollar chip falls to the floor. "It's from the Dunes," she says, picking it up.

"Too bad the Dunes went bust," he says. "We could use the money."

"Should we go through all of these, though? I'd hate to throw away anything of value."

Harlan knows there will be money in the condo, and jewelry, too. As a girl, Sarah hid everything — cigarette packs in her underwear drawer, twenty-dollar bills between the pages of teen magazines. He'd rifle through her room when she was out on a date, his only way of being close to her once the boys started to come around.

Now, with only the weekend to empty the place, he knows they can't go through everything. Marlene will fly home in the morning.

"Just open the ones you have a feeling about," he says finally. "Use your intuition."

She gives a laugh. "I seem to remember you calling my intuition bullshit."

Harlan remembers saying it. Still, it's hard to believe he was ever that unappreciative. There was a time when he was certain Marlene had a special sense for things — which mechanic to trust with the Buick, when to plant tulip bulbs. But when her intuition told her it was time for a new life without him, he came to hate the idea of intuition altogether.

"Just do what you think is best," he says, and carries two bulging trash bags to the door. His ankles throb. Basketball ankles. They're going to give him hell before the weekend is over.

There is the kitchen and one back bedroom to clear, along with a small blue-carpeted den that has been overrun by cats. Marlene refers to it as the Cat Den, and each time Harlan opens the door a dozen snarling cats dart to their hiding places under the bed. They are lean and angry, and Harlan will have to put every one of them into carrier boxes tomorrow, in order to take them to the SPCA. He'll do this after Marlene has flown home, since she hates the idea of it.

In the phone book, he finds a place that will deliver an industrial-size dumpster outside the door, and once it arrives everything moves more quickly. Load by load, the condominium becomes less cluttered, more the kind of place where any normal woman might live. Seeing the carpet and the bare white walls, Harlan feels almost as if he's curing his sister after the fact, though occasionally he's laid out by the sight of some object she loved — a beaded necklace or a mother-of-pearl-inlaid comb. Almost all of it goes into the dumpster. A stab of guilt moves through Harlan each time he throws away something she valued.

Marlene is in the kitchen, emptying cabinets, losing herself in the work. She hums Van Morrison's "Caravan," a familiar sound that puts Harlan in mind of better days. He thinks with vague despair of the night they will spend at the hotel, both of them self-conscious and awkward.

Outside, the neighborhood is hot and sun drenched. On a dead lawn across the street, two Asian boys spin the wheel of an upside-down ten-speed bike. Harlan throws the last of the ice-cream tubs into the dumpster, then turns and sees a pretty red-haired woman coming across the street. She waves in a friendly, sympathetic way, dressed in a black knee-length skirt and a white blouse.

"Were you a friend of hers?" she calls.

"Her brother," he says. "Did you know her, too?"

"A little," she says, and steps up onto the lawn. "I'm not sure if anyone here knew her, really. She was always nice to me, though." The woman's face is full of grim understanding.

"You live in the complex?"

"Across the street." She points to a unit in the middle of the block. "Sarah used to sit on her lawn right here and drink a diet root beer. We'd talk sometimes. She always loved to talk. She had a vivid imagination."

"She had problems," Harlan says, carefully.

"I didn't mind," the woman says. "I thought she was sweet. She mentioned you a couple of times, if I'm not mistaken. Are you Harlan?"

Harlan feels a sudden rush of pride, as he did when Sarah's girl-hood friends used to talk to him. "I am."

"Audrey," the woman says, and they shake hands. "It's funny, I would have guessed you were younger, the way she talked about you. I'd have put you at about twenty or so."

"It's probably how she thought of me," he says. "I think of my-self that way sometimes." He has noticed the woman's legs, which are freckled and lovely. He has to keep from staring at them. "You work at one of the casinos?"

"The Sands," she says. "One of the worst ones, actually. They're about to tear it down. I'm trying to get a job as a dealer." She glances over her shoulder at the Strip, where lights are blinking on as the sky darkens. "I'm told they like tall girls."

"You'd be perfect," he says. "I'd sit at your table."

"So what do you do? Back in — what is it? Arizona?"

"I'm a writer," he says.

"Wow, impressive. What kinds of things do you write about?"

"Mostly celebrity profiles and interviews." In fact, Harlan is a technical writer and works for a company that makes LCD panels. He has never lied about it before.

"I'll bet you know famous people," she says.

"I've met them," he says. "That's different from knowing them."

She nods, seeming to appreciate the difference. "Sarah talked about knowing famous people — Jerry Lewis, Johnny Carson. I didn't believe her at the time, but she must have met them through you."

"A few of them." Harlan wishes he could take it all back.

"She said you had the best tenor voice she ever heard in her life," the woman says.

"When did she say that?"

"She told me that a number of times. She said you'd sing 'Wild Is the Wind' in the shower and hit all the high notes, which im-pressed me. I've tried to sing that song."

"I never even knew she heard me," he says. "She was the en-tertainer in the family."

"And you have a younger brother? Hap? Happy?"

"Actually, no. Hap died when we were only kids."

"I'm sorry. I didn't know."

"It's been a difficult time," he says, then realizes how little sense he's making. He glances at the condo. "I should get back. There's a lot of work to do."

"I'd offer to help if I didn't have my shift," she says.

"I wouldn't let you, though. It's bad in there."

She smiles a sad, knowing smile. "She loved those cats," she says.

"That's right," he says. "The cats were a problem."

"Well, good luck," she says.

He watches her turn and walk down the sidewalk, her heels clicking on the concrete.

Inside, he rubs his ankles, sitting on a crushed velvet ottoman. A striped cat bounds into the room, then sees Harlan and stops, its panicky eyes frozen for a moment before it darts back down the hall.

"So who's the redhead?" Marlene asks.

"A friend of Sarah's. They used to talk sometimes."

"She's attractive."

Harlan can't keep from smiling. "Sarah told her I had the best tenor voice she'd ever heard." He stands and tests his ankles. "I guess she must have heard me in the shower."

He goes to the dining table, where Marlene is leafing through a stack of old photos. She hands him an eight-by-ten of Sarah in a powder-blue bikini, standing in front of the fountains of Caesar's Palace. One of her legs is cocked behind her, à la Betty Grable.

"What the heck is that from?"

"Pretty swank, huh?" She hands him another: Sarah in a low-cut sundress, holding a white parasol. Harlan gives a low whistle.

"They're call sheets," Marlene says. "They're for modeling and things. I was just wondering who would have paid to have them done. They're expensive."

He leafs through a few more: Sarah leaning against the shining hood of a glitter-gold Corvette; posing in front of the Stork Club in an evening dress.

"Eddie, maybe," he says. "He got on that kick where he wanted to make her a star. Any of those guys, though — Goldberg, Do-mini. They all had big bucks."

Harlan thinks of the men Sarah dated during her first years in Vegas, gangstery club owners and businessmen, older guys with silver hair, stickpins, and ruby rings. Eddie Depaolo was actually her husband for two years, though they were together only half that time. He installed her in a pink stucco mansion, and they had cocktail and dinner parties nearly every weekend. The thought of Sarah as a homemaker was hilarious to Harlan, who couldn't imagine her cooking a meal or serving anyone. God knows she never cooked when he and Marlene came to town. Instead, Eddie would take them all to Caesar's Palace, where they'd be "comped" lavish meals through Eddie's mysterious connections. "Just get the tip, kid," Eddie would say, not realizing forty bucks was more than Harlan, a kid just out of college, could afford.

Marlene is handing him more photographs: Sarah in a full-length sable coat; wearing lime-green hot pants; riding a carousel horse at a carnival. There are dinner-table shots of Sarah and at-tractive men, casino magnates with pearly, capped teeth. Harlan hated these guys, and he hated Sarah's attitude when they were around, the way her tone seemed to say, "We're with important people, Harly, don't mess up." It made him think of the Maricopa High days, with those greasy-haired athletes coming to the door. Boys he'd later overhear laughing about Sarah at school, mimick-ing the sounds she made having sex — or so he gathered. When they saw him, they buckled over, laughing into their fists. The humiliation of it stayed with him for years.

"Look, here's one of your father," Marlene says.

Harlan takes the snapshot, sees a man with close-set, dark eyes. He's in front of a drained swimming pool, pretending he's about to dive in. His hands are folded and his knees are bent. The shot is taken from below, as if the person holding the camera were a child. Harlan can't remember taking it or even a time when his father looked so jovial, so benign. He hands the photo back to Marlene, and she buries it in the pile.

"Look, here's one of Happy." She gives it to him. Dressed in overalls and a button-down shirt, Hap grins at the camera.

"Jeez, what a kid," Harlan says, and a rush of happiness overtakes him. This would be the time to go back to, he thinks, if such a thing were possible. Go back to Hap, for crying out loud, and with a little luck things might work out fine from there.

They work until Harlan's ankles swell to the size of softballs. They clear the living room, the dining room, both bedrooms, and the kitchen; they empty the cupboards and closets and strip the tinfoil and posters from the walls. Only the Cat Den remains, along with a few details that will be handled by professionals — exterminators, carpet layers, painters. Harlan will buy cat carriers at a pet shop and take the animals to the SPCA in the morning. He has started a list so he can check everything off. He has always found lists comforting.

Minutes before they leave, Marlene finds a diamond ring in the freezer, wadded in Saran wrap, tucked into an empty ice tray. She gasps as she uncovers it. The stone is nearly the size of an M&M.

Harlan hurries over and studies it under the kitchen light. He remembers the man who gave it to Sarah, Heinrich something, a tall German banker who favored bow ties and wire-rimmed glasses.

"It's gotta be two carats at least," he says.

"I've never seen anything like it," she says. "My God, I almost tossed it out with the frozen dinners!"

"You could buy some Lean Cuisine with that baby," he says.

"I bet you could," she says.

"You should keep it," he says, and feels a sudden warmth in his belly, as if he's the hotshot for once in his life, the club owner, the banker. "It'll cover your expenses."

"I'm not keeping it, Harlan," she says.

"Why not?"

"I don't want it. It's not mine."

"Come on." He takes her hand and tries to slide the still-cold ring onto her finger, laughing as she protests, even as she tries to pull her hand away. Finally she jerks it hard and says, "For Christ sakes, Harlan. I don't want it, okay? Can't you listen?"

He glances at the open freezer, at the frozen meals in the sink. "I'm sorry," he says. "I guess I didn't understand."

"I guess not," she says. She sets the ring on the counter, washes her hands at the sink, and goes down the hall to find her purse.

They drive past the Bellagio as jets of lighted water shoot above the Romanesque pools. A crowd has gathered. Old women stand with their faces upturned, the beaded lights playing across their spectacles. In front of Treasure Island a volcano erupts. To Harlan, all the glitz seems intended to hide the fact that his sister has died in a cluttered condominium half a mile away and that they are all dying, slowly and quickly, everyone inside and outside his rented Mercury. With the possible exception of a brief trip to meet with a realtor, he knows he will never visit Las Vegas again.

As he pulls under the enormous Circus Circus clown, he feels small and foolish. He has booked the cheapest room in the cheapest hotel in all of Las Vegas because, he thinks, that is the kind of half-assed Henry he is. And now, stepping out of the car, walking through the desert air, he tells himself, You've got to do better than that. You've got to stop living a life of failure.

They wait for a key at the reception desk while the slot machines ring all around them. The lobby is overrun with Shriners, most of them wearing maroon fezzes and sport coats. A group of them sit on a couch behind Harlan and Marlene, playing kazoos. Harlan watches a blind man tap his way toward a row of nickel slot machines. He holds a bucketful of coins.

"The spectacle of the human condition," says Marlene.

"I can't believe we used to like this place," he says.

"We smell awful," she whispers, sniffing his shoulder. "You can see people cringe when they smell us."

The hotel clerk returns, and Harlan watches her wince.

As they walk through the casino, Marlene says, "We'll have to burn our clothes or bury them, one or the other."

She has always been able to make him smile, even at the most unbearable times. He met her in the ASU library his junior year, when he was studying differential equations, a subject that brought him close to despair. She sat down across from him, a playful glint in her eye, and said, "That bad, huh?" Now he's happy to be able to spend a night with her, even as a friend. Having a meal together, watching a movie — these are the simple things he misses.

They take a mirrored elevator to the eighteenth floor. Their room is at the end of the hall: red curtains and a pink-and-white bedspread; two oil paintings of sad-faced clowns.

"Not exactly high rollers, are we?" he says.

"Not this time around."

Her demeanor has changed. She avoids his gaze now, glances at the phone on the night table. He is sure she wants to call the boyfriend.

"You mind if I use the shower first?" he asks.

"That'd be fine."

As he crosses the room, he feels as if his insides might fall out onto the floor. He runs the shower in the bathroom and lets the room fill with steam. Then he puts an ear to the door and listens: the sweet tones of her voice, her laughter. He is hearing the beginning of something.

He is awake most of the night, kicking the coarse hotel sheets. When the sun finally brightens the curtains, he is almost relieved. He eases his throbbing ankles to the floor and winces into the bathroom.

He has been thinking about a conversation he had with his sister five months ago. She called to tell him someone had broken into the condo.

"They took my hairbrush!" she said, her voice shrill and taut with panic. "They took some vitamin C's and a great big box of Ritz crackers. I'm afraid they're still in the house somewhere."

"No one wants your crackers," Harlan said. "They're not in the house, Sarah." He'd been eating a plate of spaghetti in front of the TV. Now he sat up and hit the mute button on the remote control.

"They'll probably wait till I'm sleeping and slit my throat," she whispered.

"Don't be melodramatic."

Through the earpiece he heard the scrape of her lighter. "They took money, too," she said, exhaling. "A lot of money."

"What money?"

"Money I *had*," she said. "*My* money."

"You just misplaced it," he said. "For all you know, the cats are hiding things under the bed."

"That's crazy," she said. "Don't say that."

"I just don't know what you expect with the place like it is."

"It's not the cats!" she shouted. "Cats don't want money!"

"All right, all right," he said "Just try and calm down."

"How can I calm down?" she said. "People break in here, Harlan. You think I don't know that? You think I don't know what *crackers* I have?" She started crying — quietly at first, then louder. The phone seemed to bump the countertop, and a long wail broke into static over the line. "Those kids come in and take my things!" she screamed into the room. He listened to her sobbing for what seemed a very long time.

Eventually she picked up the phone again, and he was able to calm her down, though it took most of the night. By the time the sky turned gray he'd convinced her that no one had broken into the condo, that no one had taken her things.

But as he steps into the shower in his Circus Circus room, a terrible thought occurs to him: What if she had been right? What if the boys who came in after she was dead had come in while she was living? What if they really *had* taken her things and her money? What if they had terrorized her?

He lets the water pull his hair down. It can't be true. His brain is moving beyond the speed of reason. He breathes in slowly, trying not to think at all. He is in a pink-tiled shower stall in a hotel in Las Vegas. His ex-wife is in the other room. These are the facts. His sister died four days ago. He is forty-one years old.

At the airport he and Marlene stand in front of her gate, waiting for her plane to board. Harlan can't stop talking.

"I should have done more," he says. "I should have insisted she see a psychiatrist."

"We tried that, Harlan," Marlene says. "She wouldn't do it."

"I should've gotten rid of the cats. It's unhealthy to breathe that."

"Sarah died of a heart attack," she says. "Her lungs had nothing to do with it."

On the car ride over, he begged her to leave the new boyfriend. He needed her, he said, and would possibly die without her. Listening to himself was like listening to a stranger — a crazy man on a city bus or in a barroom. There seemed nothing he could do to stop it.

"I can't even say for sure that I loved her," he says now. "That's the thing. I didn't even like her most of the time."

"Come on, Harlan. Let's not do this." Marlene glances at the gate counter, where the check-in agent has announced general boarding.

"I was mad at her after she moved out and left me alone with Dad," he says.

"I have to go," she says.

He wants to ask her what will become of him, because he feels as if she knows. He has come to rely on Marlene for solace, for absolution. Now she will give him neither.

What she gives him is a hug and a quick, sisterly peck on the cheek. He watches her turn and walk toward the gate door. It is hard not to think of her arriving in Phoenix, where the tall, smiling Ron will be waiting to meet her. Meanwhile, he'll be at Sarah's chasing the cats.

He smells Marlene's cinnamon-scented perfume as she walks to the gate. It is still in the air long after she's gone.

In the Cat Den he tears foil from the windows and opens them to the desert air. The room is small and so filled with clutter that it's impossible to tell what's underneath it all. The cat smell makes his eyes water. He puts on gloves and begins to stuff clothes and urine-soaked newspapers into Hefty bags, flushing several cats out of their hiding places as he works. Most of them dart under the bed, where they mewl and hiss. There might be two dozen cats under there.

The rest of the house is empty, a surprise each time Harlan sees it. The only thing left in the kitchen is the diamond ring, which he folds into a piece of pink tissue paper and stuffs in his pocket. He hauls load after load from the Cat Den, uncovering an armoire, a dresser, a rolltop desk. They are all made of a beautiful mahogany that has been horribly warped by cat urine. They must have come from the Eddie Depaolo house, though Harlan can't remember seeing them there. Inside each drawer is a small black heart, burned into the wood, with the words *fait à la main.*

By the time the sun touches the horizon, Harlan has hauled most of the debris outside. The work is slow, and he can't get through the door without tripping over a cat or being scratched. His wrists are streaked with thin red lines. So far he has managed to get only two cats into the carriers, and both of them scream and paw the grates without ceasing.

He takes a breather at the window, watching a jet rise from Vegas Airport, its navigation lights flashing red and white. Marlene will be back in Phoenix by now. Harlan realizes with a flash of shame that he didn't thank her for coming. It's typical of him — going on like a child, whining about his guilt. She's better off without him, no question about it.

A motorcycle speeds past, the rider bent low over the gas tank. Harlan sees the Asian boys across the street, sitting on the same dead lawn, smoking cigarettes. They are older than he imagined, fifteen or so. And as they flick their cigarette butts into the yard, a thought occurs to him: what if they are the boys who came into the condo? It is a reckless notion, completely unsubstantiated, but just as he thinks it the boys turn and see him in the window, and their expressions seem to confirm it: they are frightened.

He calls out to them, and they scramble to their feet, picking up two red ten-speeds in the driveway. By the time Harlan reaches the yard, they are halfway down the block, standing on their pedals, pumping hard. He calls again but they don't even turn around.

"Bastards," he says.

He looks at the flat brown lawn across the street. The condo is a duplicate of Sarah's, but with the carport on the opposite side. He crosses the street and reads the name on the mailbox — Ng. Vietnamese. He realizes he didn't suspect the boys because of their ethnicity and wonders what sort of prejudice that is. He rings the doorbell, but no one answers. Through a gap in the blinds he sees a dark living room, a yellow bird flapping in a cage.

He remembers the red-haired woman, Audrey, and considers trying to find her, but what would he say if he did? *I know I smell like the insides of a cat, but I may have found some boys who smoked cigarettes in my dead sister's condominium.* What could she do about it anyway? The police know what happened and have taken no interest. Harlan limps back across the street.

In the Cat Den, an orange tabby the size of a beagle stands near the closet, raising its hackles at Harlan and snarling.

"How'd you like to get put in a box?" he asks it.

The cat takes a step forward, its agate eyes on the door.

"If you want to leave, leave," Harlan says. "You think I care?" He rushes the cat, and it streaks past him into the hallway.

Another cat shoots out from under the bed, and Harlan shoos that one into the hallway, too, then goes to the bed and yanks the bedsprings up with both hands. Cats dart in every direction, an explosion of cats: tabbies and toms, all colors and sizes. They tear the carpet trying to get away. Shuffle-stepping toward the door, he scares them into the living room. "Everybody moves!" he shouts. "Everybody rallies!" He picks up a broom and sweeps the slower ones down the hall.

The front door is open, and a lot of cats have gotten out already. Harlan steps outside and chases them across the yard.

As they vanish under bushes and behind parked cars, he feels better than he has all weekend. He should have thought of this yesterday — just letting the cats fend for themselves. They'll have a better chance in the wild than they'd have at the pound, and God knows it's the easiest solution for Harlan. For the first time he feels as if he'll finish his work and make it back to the hotel room. He'll shower and have dinner at one of the casinos, maybe plunk a few dollars into the slots. If he wants, he can even book the room for another night. It is a city of fast-changing fortunes, after all. His luck can't get much worse than it has been.

But as he chases a black cat out of the yard, he sees the two Asian boys round the corner, weaving slowly on their bikes. A girl on roller skates struggles to keep up with them, her blond hair blowing back over her shoulders. Harlan's first impulse is to duck behind a palm tree and pretend he hasn't seen them, then slip unseen into the condo once they're gone. But something — the memory of Sarah's phone call, maybe, her strained, hysterical voice — swells his chest with anger. He turns and runs as fast as he can in the boys' direction.

The girl is the first to see him coming. She calls out to the boys, who hit their brakes and try to get the bikes turned around. Harlan goes after the smaller of the two, who manages to pop up onto the curb and rattle over a lawn. When Harlan gets hold of his seat post, the boy scrambles off the bike and runs. Harlan goes after him, ankles burning. He has no plan except to stop the boy, to keep him from getting away. Twenty feet down the road, he reaches out and grabs the boy's black T-shirt and holds it tight.

"Turn around," he shouts. "Don't make me tear this thing."

The boy turns. His eyes are sharp and insolent. He spits on the pavement and shouts something in Vietnamese.

"Did you go in there?" Harlan asks him. "Did you go into her house?"

The kid jerks his shirttail back and looks up the street. The girl is coming on her skates.

"What's your problem?" she yells at Harlan, skidding to a stop.

"They went into my sister's house," he says. He turns to the boy. "Tell her what you did in there."

The boy glares at him, his upper lip curling. "Fut you," he says.

Harlan imagines taking the boy's skinny neck in his hands and squeezing. The thought sends a thrill through his body.

The rattle of a bike chain comes from behind, and he turns and sees the other boy riding in, a wooden croquet mallet in one hand. It takes a moment for Harlan to understand what's happening. The boy swoops in, raising the mallet like a polo player, and Harlan has to duck and turn to keep from getting cracked on the skull.

"My God," he shouts, as the boy pedals away. "You're crazy!"

The smaller boy is crouched in front of him, fists cocked, eyes flicking around. The boy steps in and tries to kick Harlan in the crotch, and Harlan barely blocks it.

"Stop it!" he shouts. "I mean it." He searches the boy's eyes for a hint of understanding.

"Kill him, Tuyen," the girl says, circling them on her skates. "Karate-chop that fucker."

Harlan hears the chain again. When he turns this time, he sees Audrey, standing on the dead lawn in front of her condo, her eyes wide. She raises a hand to Harlan, and he waves back. But suddenly the boy is upon him, the mallet coming down. Harlan feels a burst of pain at his temple, and the sky flashes white for an instant. His legs buckle. A breath of wind passes through his hair. The first thing he feels upon waking is the hot pavement beneath his cheek.

He tries to raise his body, but his brain tips like the ball of a compass. He hears Audrey's heels clacking over the pavement.

"My God," she says, crouching down beside him. "You're really hurt, aren't you?"

"They came into the condo," he says. "Or I think they did."

She helps him to a sitting position. The boys are at the end of the block, rounding the corner. Audrey touches the side of his head, where the pain thrums like a heart. With the Strip behind her, she could almost be an angel, her eyes bright, her hair filled with red and gold. Harlan sees Sarah's condo across the street — the door open, the living room empty. All this really happened, he thinks, amazed. It's as if he's understanding it for the first time, as if the pain has taken away his guilt and allowed his grief to finally bloom.

A car is coming. He has to stand, which is no easy task. Audrey helps him to his feet. They take tiny steps across the blacktop.

In her condo, she leads him to a long white couch. The scent of lilies comes from somewhere in the room. The condo is so bright and clean it's impossible to believe it's an exact replica of Sarah's.

"I'll get something for your cut," she says, and goes down the hall.

He looks through the front window at Sarah's, seeing it as Audrey has seen it: the ruined lawn, the naked-looking windows, the dumpster overflowing with Hefty bags. He can remember coming here for the first time thirteen years ago, when the palm in the yard was no taller than he was. It was the day after his wedding. Sarah wanted to take him and Marlene to the Stork Club for their first lunch as newlyweds. She'd come to the wedding in Valentino and pearls and had made a big impression on Marlene, who was meeting her for the first time. Harlan wanted to show his sister off again.

But when he knocked at her door, it was several minutes before she answered, and then she was dressed in a terry-cloth robe and slippers, her hair a wild tangle atop her head. Despite her elaborate excuses about a Mexican alarm clock, Harlan knew she had simply forgotten about the lunch. That was Sarah: capable of throwing a great light on your life, then completely forgetting you. As she got ready in the bedroom — a process that took nearly two hours — Harlan turned to Marlene and said, "Now you've really met my sister."

Audrey comes back with a washcloth and first-aid kit. She sits on the couch beside Harlan.

"That was my mallet," she says, and gives him a wry smile. "I just realized. The thing he hit you with. I must have left it in the yard." She puts a hand to his cheek. "So this is all my fault."

"No," he says.

"Turn your head, now. This might sting."

It does. On the street, Harlan sees a black cat slink out from under a pickup truck.

"I'd like to catch those cats," he says, and thinks suddenly of what they'll go through, surviving for the first time on instincts dulled by years indoors. "They got out. Or I chased them out. I shouldn't have done that."

"Hold still," she says, and continues her painful ministrations.

As he washes his face with Audrey's almond-scented hand soap, he's reminded of how awful *he* must smell — even worse than yesterday, since he's been working in the Cat Den. A rush of embarrassed gratitude comes over him, because she has given no indication of noticing. He dries his face, then reaches into his pocket for Sarah's diamond ring. He unravels it from the tissue and sets it on the counter beside a dish filled with potpourri. It feels good to pass on something of Sarah's, especially after throwing so much away. He imagines it's what his sister would have wanted him to do.

Audrey rises from the sofa when he comes out. He attempts to smile at her.

"I'm so sorry for the —" he almost says "smell" but stops

himself "— for everything, really. I must seem like a disaster, crashing into your life on a Saturday."

"I was very glad to meet you," she says, her face a perfect balance of gravity and assurance. "It's too bad you had to get hit over the head with my mallet."

"It is."

"And I'm really sorry about Sarah."

Harlan's eyes begin to tear. He mumbles his thanks, shakes her hand, and walks out the front door.

Above the cinder-block wall surrounding the complex, the Strip is lighted like a beacon for those desperate enough to follow. He'll follow it as far as Circus Circus, but only to shower and have a meal. In the morning he'll fly back to Phoenix. He imagines Audrey finding the ring in the bathroom. Already, it seems an embarrassing gesture, the crazy act of a crazy woman's brother.

He cleans up quickly, not wanting to be there if she comes to return the ring. There are only a few more loads to haul now, and no cats to impede his progress. The final load is a Hefty bag of stinking throw rugs, and once it is in the dumpster he walks back inside and goes from room to room, looking at the bare walls, checking the closets and cupboards. Here are the rooms where his sister lived, where she was a waitress and a showgirl and a lunatic. He can't get out of there fast enough.

As he's locking up, he hears a meow from the kitchen and sees a cat come out, small and gray, with patches of black on its paws. It stares at him — not wildly like the others, but in a timid, curious way. It glances at the open door, then at him.

"I don't know," he says. "I think we just have to leave."

He steps back from the door and lets the cat go through. As it ambles across the grass, it is touched, like everything else, by the glow of the Strip. Harlan steps out, locks the door, and follows it over the lawn.

Why the Sky
Turns Red
When the Sun
Goes Down

―――――

I get the call as my wife is setting the table for dinner. It's our neighbor, Ben Hildeman, who tells me in a breathless voice that my son has had a problem.

"This is bad, Mike," Ben says, and in the background I hear his boys, Tanner and Phillip, talking in excited tones. "He fell and hurt his leg, is what happened first, I guess, and then he just sort of lost control. By the time I got there he was in the Kohlers' yard, banging his head against their air-conditioning unit."

"God, you're kidding," I say.

"I'm afraid it's pretty bad, Mike. Some of the kids are upset now. I wish you'd come down."

"I'll be right there," I say, and hang up the phone.

Dana comes into the doorway with a bunch of utensils in her hand. "It's not about Cole?" she says, but she can see in my face that it is. "You should go, Mike. Hurry."

As I run down Keehouatupa, past the subterranean houses, I'm hoping that whatever happened to Cole will have nothing to do with the trouble we had in Portland. I know Dana is thinking the same thing back at the house. We came to Arizona at the height of the D3 crisis, with high hopes that the desert air would be good for Cole, and amazingly, in the seven months we've been here, he's not had a single problem — no shutdown or twitching hands, no problems with speech or movement. We'd only just begun to believe that things might be all right again.

Ben's house comes into view, a newly built subterranean with smoke-tinted skylights, a couple of date palms shimmering above it in the day's waning heat. Ben stands on the grassy dome, a stocky man in sweatpants. Behind him are the red peaks of the Superstition Mountains. Half a dozen boys stand on either side of him in shorts and tank tops. Cole, I see, is not among them.

Ben jogs down and puts a hand on my shoulder. "I didn't want to touch him, Mike," he says. "He's around back now. I think he might be unconscious."

"That's good, actually. It means he's in shutdown."

We run up the hill. From the top, I see Cole lying belly-down on the back slope, his legs splayed out behind him. He *is* in shutdown — there's that stillness about him — and I'm relieved to see it, though it's clear he's in horrible shape. His neck has twisted around so far that his chin rests in the valley between his shoulder blades. His right arm has come off completely. It lies, bent at the elbow, a few yards away, multicolored wires curling out of the torn end. I get a light-headed feeling and have to crouch for a moment and catch my breath.

"You all right?" Ben asks.

"I'll be okay."

"He just —" Ben gives me a squint-eyed look. "It's hard to describe it, Mike. It was crazy."

"So all this happened when he fell? The arm and everything?"

"That's what I was saying." He jerks a thumb toward a metal box at the edge of the Kohlers' yard. "When I came out he was just banging against that thing like he wanted to knock it down or something. He made an electrical noise in his throat, sort of a whirring sound."

I glance at the boys, who are all studying me carefully — six boys in a line on the hill.

"Everybody all right?" I ask.

They nod.

"I asked them to go home, but they wouldn't go," Ben says. "They're worried about their friend."

"Sure," I say. "Well, listen, guys, Cole's gonna be all right, you hear?"

They nod again and glance at one another. These are good kids, all of them — Ben's son Tanner and our next-door neighbor, Sean Ho, and a Devin something whose parents I've met a few times. One of them, a red-haired boy I haven't seen before, looks as though he might be D3 himself; his skin seems to reflect the sun a little more directly than the other boys', and he holds his shoulders unusually straight. Most people can't tell the difference, but the parents of D3 kids can more often than not. This kid looks as stunned as the rest of them.

I walk down the grassy slope and kneel beside Cole. His eyes are wide open and staring at nothing, and that's something I hate to see. I lay a hand on each of his cheeks, turn his head to the side and feel a pop — his neck feels looser than it should. I brush his bangs from his forehead, roll him to his back, and slip a hand under his T-shirt, feeling for the power button. I give it a push.

Cole's head jerks just slightly. His eyes change, almost imperceptibly, as if the dimmest light has gone on behind them. It's enough, though: he looks like my son again.

"Hey, buddy," I say.

He blinks at me. "Hey, Dad. What are you doing here?"

"I came to take you home."

He glances around. I see the disappointment in his eyes, the look of understanding. "I had an accident," he says.

"I'm afraid so. Do you remember anything that happened?"

"We were playing Kick the Can," he says, and draws his lips in, concentrating. "I was running, I think. I had a bad headache. I don't remember anything else."

"That's all right."

I'm relieved he's come out of it alert and lucid, much better than times in the past. During the bad period in Portland there were always problems upon switchback—inability to focus, slowed-down speech and movement.

"So listen, there are a few things I need to tell you," I say. "Things you may not want to hear." I help him to a sitting position, a hand at the small of his back. "For one thing, your arm's come off."

He touches his shoulder where the arm should be. A look of panic overtakes him.

"It's all right," I say. "It's just down the hill. We'll get it fixed up as soon as we can. I just want you to know what's going on. The other thing is that I think there might be a little problem with your neck, but that'll be fine, too, I promise."

He swallows hard. "What about my arm?" he says. "Aren't you going to put in on again?"

"I can't, pal. I wish I could. We'll have to bring it along to the hospital tomorrow."

He glances up at his friends on the hill. I know he's embarrassed about what's happened.

"Maybe you ought to say something to them," I tell him. "Let them know you're all right."

"I don't know what to say."

"Just whatever you want. It'll make it easier when you see them the next time."

He thinks for a moment, his tongue poking out between his lips. Then he glances up the hill and calls, "Hey, guys, I'm all right and everything. I gotta go home, but I can probably come back tomorrow."

"Hey, that's terrific," Ben says, and glances around at the boys. "Isn't that great, guys?"

"Yeah," Tanner Hildeman says quietly. "That's great, Cole."

"We just hope you're okay and everything," Sean says, then glances at Cole's arm where it lies on the grass. He turns to the other kids, and as if given a signal they all start down the hill. A couple of them raise their hands to Cole, and Cole waves back.

"That wasn't so bad, was it?"

"I guess not," he says.

"You ready to go home to Mom now?"

"All right," he says, but there's a hint of hesitation in his eyes.

"What is it?" I ask.

He shakes his head. "Does Mom know what happened?"

"She knows you got hurt," I tell him. "She'll be glad to see you."

He glances up at the date palms in front of the house.

"What's the matter, buddy?"

"Nothing," he says, but I can see that something's wrong. For the first time I realize he must know more about Dana and me than we've imagined.

———

Dana is outside when we get home, standing at the edge of the lawn, an uneasy look on her face. I give her a reassuring nod, but there's little use in that with Cole's arm tucked under my own like a rolled-up newspaper.

"Oh boy," she says, glancing from Cole to me and back. "You all right, kid?"

"I guess," he says.

"He's disappointed," I say.

"Of course. Who wouldn't be?" She brushes her hands down her sides. Dana is an attorney at an intellectual property firm in Phoenix. She makes a good living appearing composed when everything is going to hell around her, but she's flustered now, and it makes me feel suddenly tender toward her. Together we go into the house, where the air is cool and smells of pork chops and mashed potatoes.

———

While Cole goes upstairs to get cleaned up, I walk into the kitchen. Dana is washing her hands in front of the big window. It's six o'clock, and the sky has taken on the pinks and silvers of an abalone shell.

"Don't you think we ought to shut him down?" she asks. "I'm not sure I can stand to see him with his arm like that."

"It's better to keep him running if we can," I say. "We don't want him to get any more disoriented than he has to."

"I guess not."

"He seems pretty good in most ways. This is probably nothing too serious."

"He's torn his own arm off, Mike," she says. "Of course it's serious."

"All right," I say. "I just mean it might be a mechanical problem. It's not necessarily anything chronic."

Her face is doubtful, weary. "Well, let's hope so," she says.

At the top of the stairs I hear the faucet running in the bathroom. Cole bumps a knee against the cabinet under the sink and says, "Ouch," then the faucet shuts off with a knock. I walk into the master bathroom, where the face I see in the mirror is so pale it shocks me. I have to sit on the toilet for a while with my head between my knees. It's that echoey feeling I had in the Hildemans' yard, a feeling I had a lot as a kid — at swim meets and at summer camp and later during final exams in college. A doctor put me on Palidex for a while when I was in my twenties, but I didn't like the way it made me feel — sedate and detached from my life. I sit blotting my forehead with toilet paper, breathing deeply until my heartbeat slows.

I had these symptoms back in Portland, too, when Cole was at his worst and Dana and I disagreed about how to handle it. Dana wanted to get a new center chip for Cole then, one of the D4 units that seemed to work well for people at the time. To me that would have been like getting a new child altogether, since his personality wouldn't have been the same. In D children, experience affects development the way it affects a human child: D children become who they are because of the lives they've lived. While it's possible to transfer memory, you can't transfer a personality that's been formed over the years. We'd been told that the engineers could *approximate* Cole's personality type, which to me was worthless, though a lot of people disagreed with me. My wife happened to be one of them.

Dana's older brother, Davis, had a D3 child of his own, a boy named Brice who suffered for years from the same kinds of problems as Cole — intermittent breakdown, loss of motor control. A year before we moved to Arizona, on the Tuesday before Thanksgiving, Brice disappeared after a martial-arts class and it was almost a week before they found him in a wooded field two miles north of Davis's house, where he'd apparently collapsed while taking a shortcut home. A week later, Davis had a new center chip installed. The results were so positive he couldn't help calling us about it during our worst stretch with Cole. He knew how I felt about center chips; we'd discussed it many times. Davis had always been protective of Dana, and I'd gotten the feeling he never quite approved of me. I began to see his calls as a way of stirring up trouble between me and Dana.

And it worked. Brice was a high school junior then, a scholar-athlete and a truly fine kid, a boy Dana and I had always liked. But it was less his personality and accomplishments that impressed Dana, I think, than the sheer absence of D3-related problems. I remember Davis being worried about drugs at one point (he'd found a marijuana cigarette in Brice's underwear drawer), and even that became a selling point, because it was a *normal* problem. You couldn't miss the pride in Davis's voice when he told us about it — about the awkward talk he'd had with Brice, the two of them hashing it out for nearly an hour before finally hugging and crying. The point seemed to be that Brice was living a life of uninterrupted normalcy, and the insinuated question was, Why settle for a child who breaks down all the time when you can have a new one who won't?

I was dead set against it. It mattered absolutely to me that Cole be *my* child, the boy I'd come to know over the years. Dana and I fought about it more than we'd ever fought about anything, and in the end it changed the way we saw each other. She came to seem harder to me, less forgiving; I must have come to seem weak and sentimental. We'd met during our final year at the University of Oregon and for the longest time had been amazed by how much we had in common — a love of old books and antiques, a respect for nature, a desire to have kids while we were still young enough to do everything with them. But as the problems with Cole grew worse, Dana receded, took on longer hours at work, and became distant when she was home. We argued about small, unrelated things, like the antiques we'd collected over the years; she felt hemmed in by them, even suggested we sell the old gas-powered Bonneville we'd loved to drive in college. For a few months that fall, I became convinced she was having an affair with a man named Stuart Solomon, a high-tech consultant at her firm. I never had solid evidence. Stuart's name showed up a few times on the caller ID, though he and Dana worked on different accounts. Twice, when Dana was supposed to be working late, I drove to her office and found her car was not in the parking lot. I tried to confront her about it but always lost my nerve. There's no describing my relief when the reports came in about D3 kids in the Southwest. Suddenly there was reason to think our lives could return to normal.

I stand and walk to the window. Outside, the rows of subterranean houses lie spread out like the fairways of a golf course. Mine is one of the few two-story houses left in the neighborhood now, and it costs so much to cool I'm sure I won't be able to keep it long — though I hate to think of giving it up, since it's a link to my past, to the two-story colonial my family still owns in Eugene. From where I stand, I can see the only other two-story on the street, a big stucco home with a pool in the back. A light goes on upstairs, and a man passes a window. I've never spoken to this man before, but I find myself thinking about him now, wondering if he's anything like me, if he feels himself being ushered into the future, away from the things that once brought him comfort.

Downstairs, Cole is carrying a basket of rolls to the table with his one good hand, singing "My Bonnie Lies over the Ocean." It's a song he learned at summer camp, but he's gotten some of the words wrong. Instead of singing "Bonnie," he sings "body." "My body lies over the ocean / My body lies over the sea." He sets the rolls on the table and goes back for more.

"Sit, honey," Dana says from the kitchen. "I'll get the rest."

"I don't mind," he says.

He takes a pitcher of water from the counter and starts into the dining room. Dana touches the back of his neck. I give her a look meant to say, "Doesn't he seem fine?" and she gives me a more doubtful look. But she comes over and puts her arms around me, an offering of peace.

"All right, break it up," Cole says, hurrying back in. "Can't you see I'm starving here?"

We bring the rest of the food to the table, and as we begin to pass dishes and talk I feel as if we've gotten past the day's bad luck and tension.

"Good dinner, Mom," Cole says, forking up a bite of pork chop.

"Flattery will get you everywhere," she says, smiling.

"Listen," I say, passing the rolls, "how'd you guys like to take the Bonneville out tomorrow? After we get everything taken care of at the hospital, we could head out to Saguaro Lake and have a picnic. Maybe drive around Tortilla Flat."

"All right," Dana says. "Sounds like a good idea."

"Cool with me," says Cole, glancing up from his plate.

Something is wrong with his eyes. One of them points directly at me while the other shoots off at a crazy angle toward the kitchen. I glance at Dana, who's noticed it, too.

"What?" Cole says, looking from me to Dana. "What's wrong?"

"Nothing," Dana says carefully. "It's just—can you see all right?"

"Yeah," he says. "Why?"

"Listen, kid, try this," I say. I put a hand in front of his face, then slowly move it until my fingers have entered the line of his wayward eye. "Can you see my fingers now?"

"No," he says, and a flash of panic comes over him. "What's happening, Dad?"

"Well, I don't think it's anything to worry about. It looks like you've lost vision in one of your eyes, is all. But we're going to the hospital tomorrow anyway, right? They can fix this in a snap."

"That's right," Dana says.

For a minute I think Cole might start to cry. "Gaw!" he says, and throws his balled-up napkin on the table. "I can't believe this!"

"Hey, come on," Dana says, her tone gentle but firm. She goes to Cole and kisses the crown of his head, and whispers, "Don't let it get you down." Then she gives me a look and walks into the kitchen.

Cole and I keep on with our dinners. When Dana's been gone for a minute, I get up and go after her. She's at the sink, staring out the window at the fading sunset.

"We've got to shut him down, Mike," she says. "This is scary. It's scaring *him*."

"I know," I say, because it's scaring me, too. I can't think of anything else to do about it.

"Hey, Dad," Cole calls from the dining room.

"Be out in a second, kid."

"Dad, what makes the sky red when the sun goes down?"

Dana breathes out a laugh, and her face softens. For a moment she looks like the young woman I met in Oregon. I give her a kiss on the cheek and go into the dining room.

"That's just dust," I say. "Dust and pollution, actually."

But Cole isn't looking at me. He's pushing food across the table with his fingers, staring at the mess he's made. An electric drone comes from his throat.

"Cole?" I say.

"I gotta go to the bathroom," he says, staring at the table. "I don't feel so hot." The drone in his throat gets louder.

"What's the matter, Cole?"

He glances up, his expression suddenly sly. "I'll bet you a dollar," he says. "I'll bet you *five* dollars."

"What are you talking about?"

Dana comes into the doorway. "What's going on, Mike?"

"Jesus H. Christ," Cole says, and laughs suddenly. "Holy frickin' shit!"

"Cole! Look up here," I say. "Look at me."

He raises his head, but his eyes veer in different directions. His jaw makes a loud clicking noise. Then he raises his head high and brings it down with a violent crack against the table.

"Cole!" I say.

He lifts his head again, his face covered with pork chop grease and broccoli. I try to get around the table to hold him down, but before I can get there his head hits the table with another crack, rattling the silverware. Dana shrieks. This time, when Cole's head comes up, it swings way back over one shoulder, loose and wild.

"My God, his neck!" Dana says.

"I see it! Help me hold him down."

I get a hand on his shoulder and try to reach under his shirt for the power button, but it's hard to get to with his head lolling around like a jack-in-the-box.

"Whoa!" he says. "Help me, Dad."

The smell of burning wires comes off him. He breathes out an electric wheeze, his head reeling back. Then his face fills with wonder, and he goes still in my arms. He cranes his head around to look at me, his eyes clear and perfectly aligned.

"This is the best Christmas ever," he says.

I shut him down. His head thumps against the table. The electric drone cuts out. I wipe his face with a napkin and then go into the kitchen, where I get a bottle of beer from the fridge. When I come back Dana is at the table, arms folded across her chest.

"That's it, Mike," she says. "I mean it. This has got to stop."

The next morning I pull the Bonneville out of the driveway and carry Cole downstairs. Even with the seat belt over his shoulder, it's hard to prop him up in a way that looks natural. His head tips forward, making his mouth fall open. Dana and I have not talked about taking the Bonneville out since last night, and a picnic no longer seems like the best idea, but I'm in the mood to feel the thrum of the big gasoline engine, the vibration of the catalytic converter under my legs.

After a few minutes, Dana comes down, and we take Highway 1073 past the mall and the hydroponics yards. The D-Pediatric is twelve miles away, a sprawling complex on the outskirts of Olberg. As we drive, Dana stares out the window, her eyes steady and serious.

Last night, after I shut Cole down and we cleaned up the mess in the dining room, Dana went into the den to call her brother, Davis, and through the door I heard her talking softly. I couldn't make out what she said, though I'm certain it was something she couldn't say to me, since we went through the evening without talking about Cole at all. Sometime late in the night I woke to the sound of her crying, and she moved into my arms for a while until she was able to sleep.

Afterward I lay awake, looking at the tiny red light of the smoke detector, listening as the wind pulled an ocotillo branch across the window. Dana was asleep, and Cole, I knew, was much farther away than that, gone in a sense, so that he was not even dreaming and would not wake up and call my name. I waited until the sky whitened in the window, then got up and walked down the hall to his room. Cole lay dressed on top of the covers, his eyes closed, an inappropriate smile on his face. I had an urge to put his pajamas on him and tuck him into bed, but I knew it wouldn't make me feel better. Eventually I just went downstairs and started coffee and made bacon and eggs.

We pass Chandler now, and the ground opens up to uncultivated fields and cacti. Just beyond Alvarado, I catch a glimpse of a coyote between the clumps of sage, golden brown and moving quickly, its nose to the ground. It makes me think of driving out to Clear Lake with Dana when we first got the Bonneville, years ago, laying a blanket across the backseat and making love right in the car with the windows open, the sound of the wind coming through the firs.

In the rearview mirror I see Cole propped against the door, his eyes closed, his mouth open. Dana is staring out the window. For some reason I imagine she's thinking of Davis, and it makes me angry.

"So suppose things get bad again," I say, and glance at her. "What do you think would happen then?"

"What do you mean?" she asks.

"Suppose this is the beginning of more bad times with Cole. We'd have to make some decisions then, right?" My voice is sharp, but it seems beyond my power to control it.

"Of course," she says.

"But you already know what you'd want to do," I say. "Isn't that right, too?"

"Come on, Mike, don't do this," she says. "I'm not in the mood for an argument right now."

"But suppose it's important for me to know where we stand on this."

She sighs, glancing out at the fields of brush. "Why do you have to push things all the time?" she asks. "I can't say what I'd do in every single situation. Can you?"

"I think I can. Yes."

"Can you, really? You can say what you'd do no matter what happens to him, or to us?"

"What do you mean 'to us'?"

"Oh, God, I don't know." She shakes her head. "I just get tired of waking from the dream. Don't you ever feel that way? Don't you get tired of being reminded he's not real?"

"He's as real to me as you are," I say, but when I glance at Cole in the rearview mirror he looks like what he is — a mechanical boy, a sophisticated doll for adults.

The desert floor is flat and runs out to a line of purple mountains. A ranch house slips past, then the solar processing plant, huge and complicated. For a moment I feel as if I don't know what matters most. Dana has closed her eyes and is leaning back against the headrest.

"There was a coyote back there in a field," I say in a small, quiet voice. "I should have pointed him out to you."

We wait for almost an hour in the small, air-conditioned lobby, sitting on a vinyl couch, trying to read magazines while other parents come and go with their kids. Finally Dr. Otsuji comes down the hall in a crisp white coat. He gives us his doctor's smile and sits on the chrome magazine table across from us.

"He's fine," he says. "We've fixed the arm and the neck, and right now he's just going through some tests to make sure everything's in good shape. He seems terrific."

Dana nods, the way she does in court when conceding a point made by the opposition.

"Do you have any idea what happened?" she asks.

The doctor looks up at the low ceiling tiles, thinking. "I'd call it an anomaly," he says, "though it could be more than that. It's like if you have arrhythmia — unless we can check your heart when it's happening, we have a hard time knowing what causes it."

"But, in your opinion, is it more likely we'll have problems?" she asks. "Now that this has happened?"

Dr. Otsuji looks from one of us to the other, as if he's noticed the tension between us. "He's not showing any symptoms that would point to that, no, but to be honest, I don't see it as a good sign. For someone with Cole's history, you want as few problems as possible. Problems can lead to problems, is one way of looking at it."

Dana nods.

"Can we see him?" I ask.

"In a few minutes. He's a little upset, as you might expect. He's had a rough day. What I'd like to do is just put him out for a few minutes and run some numbers, then let him wake up naturally. I'll have the receptionist tell you when you can see him." He smiles in his professional way, then stands, shakes our hands, and walks down the hall.

"Well, there it is," I say.

"I should call Davis," Dana says, and takes her bag up from the floor. "He'll want to know what happened."

She opens her cell phone, but before dialing she looks at me with an expression I've never seen before, her face hard, her eyes narrowed with what appears to be pity. It's as if she's far away and needs to squint just to see me. "Listen," she says, "if you still want to go for a drive, that's fine. We can do that later."

"Forget it. I don't really feel like it now."

"Well. Whatever. We'll go if you want to."

"I said I don't."

The tone of my voice silences us. She stands and goes down the hall to call Davis.

Outside, clouds move across the sky, changing the light. A young family rushes into the lobby, the man carrying a blond, catatonic-looking girl in his arms. The child stares straight ahead with vacant eyes. I pick up a magazine, but there's no use trying to read or even think about anything before I'm able to see Cole. Finally, after a long ten minutes, the receptionist calls my name. I get Cole's room number and go down the hall.

Cole's in a bed in a pale-yellow hospital gown, asleep with his arms at his sides. His cheeks are flushed, his hair a little tousled. I stand above him and watch his chest rise and fall. He opens his eyes, glances around, and nods in a resigned way. "The hospital," he says.

"I'm afraid so, pal. They've fixed your arm, though. Check it out."

He raises the arm and rolls his shoulder. I see he's trying to appear calm for my sake. His eyes are wide and alert.

"Does it feel all right?"

"Pretty good," he says.

"We'll test it out with a game of catch," I say. "I brought the Bonneville. Maybe we can drop your mom off at home, then head out to Hopi Park. We'll just grab some mitts and go."

"Where *is* Mom?" he says, with a worried look.

"Down the hall. Talking to your Uncle Davis."

"Is she mad at me?"

"Of course not. Why do you say that?"

"I know she doesn't like it when I break down all the time."

"You don't break down all the time. And anyway, everyone knows it's not your fault."

"I guess," he says.

He's distracted, as if he's trying to listen for Dana's voice down the hall. I can just hear her talking, a low, familiar sound coming over the tiles.

"Let's get you dressed and get your hair combed," I say. "We don't want people to think you were raised by wolves."

He lifts the covers and lowers his legs to the floor. I help him with the ties at the back of his gown. His clothes are on a chair by the window. As he puts them on I see the seam where his arm has been reattached, a thin band where the skin is a little lighter, nothing you'd notice unless you were a parent or a doctor. I comb his hair, crouching in front of him, watching his eyes, which are alive with private thoughts and worries.

"Now you look like a gentleman," I say. "You ready to go?"

"I guess so," he says, and together we walk out into the hall.

On the ride home we play a game called Blackout. The object is to find the letters of each other's name in the license plates of passing cars, then call them out before the other person does. If you call them all, the person is out of the game. There's very little traffic until we hit the highway, and then we're suddenly in a sea of sedans and SUVs. Cole picks up a D for Dana and an M for Mike. I get A for Dana, who seems not to be paying attention.

"You better hurry up, Mom," Cole says, leaning over the front seat. "You've got two letters already."

She gazes straight out the windshield. Ever since our exchange at the hospital, she's been stiff and far away. I've seen the effect on Cole, the way he keeps trying to draw her attention.

"There's an I, Dad," he says, and points at a yellow Omni. He glances at Dana.

We get off the highway and drive down De la Sol, past the golf course and the hydroponics yards. At a red light, I call an O and an N, and then Cole and I both see a Honda in front of us, the license plate ALA-36940. We meet each other's gaze in the mirror, but neither of us calls the A.

At home I pull into the driveway and kill the engine. Dana steps out of the car. She pretends not to hear Cole when he asks if she's coming to the park with us. He watches her walk to the house.

"She's having a rough time," I say, "but she'll be all right."

He nods, his face tight and willfully composed.

"I'll go get the mitts," I say. "We'll have a good time, you'll see."

Inside, Dana sits at the dining table, staring out the window. The sky has burst into color and filled the room with light.

"So what's the plan?" I ask. "Treat him badly? Make him feel like he doesn't have a mom?"

She glances up. I see that her cheeks are wet from crying. "Are you really going to do this?" she asks. "Would you really take him and leave me alone?"

"Well, I guess I don't know what my legal options are."

"No one said anything about legal options, Mike," she says, "though I shouldn't be surprised if you're thinking in that direction." She gives her head a shake and looks at me in a surprisingly open way, her eyes soft and even. "If I try hard enough, I can almost imagine how I look to you right now."

"Can you really?"

"Yes, I can," she says. "And it's not pretty, I know. I'm sorry."

"I don't think either of us looks very good to the other right now." I try a smile, sitting across from her, breathing in her citrusy perfume.

"I was so in love with you," she says, and puts a hand on top of mine, looking me in the eye. "You know that, I hope. I still love you very much."

"I love you, too," I say, and let out a laugh, because it all seems so crazy. "It's not as if we've lost everything, though, is it? It's not as if everything's gone."

"I don't know," she says. "Sometimes I'm afraid it is."

Cole and I drive out Clementine Road, past orange groves and fields of yuccas. The air is warm through the windows. Cole takes his mitt up from the floorboard and socks the ball into the pocket. He's been quiet since I got back to the car but seems to be cheering up now under the influence of the drive. We pass an old stable building, the wood planks faded to silver. He asks if I remember a drive we took a couple of winters ago, when it hailed so hard we had to pull over and wait for it to stop.

"We were on our way to see the rodeo," I recall.

"I thought the hail would dent the roof," he says. "There was a little dog out in the street, remember? You went out and brought him into the car."

"I remember he smelled like garbage."

"He did not," he says, excited. He seems to be coming to the point of his story, which I think will be that he should be allowed to have a dog, an argument he's been making lately. Before he can get to that, though, the fingers of his right hand begin to jump, and he slips them into his mitt. It's not like him to hide anything from me. He stares straight ahead as we pass the arboretum and the reservoirs.

I can't stop thinking of Dana, thinking she's become a different person again, even more distant than she was when we lived in Portland. Of course, we'll both have to be different people if we intend to go our separate ways. Our conversation has made it necessary to imagine caring for Cole by myself, something I've not considered in months. I imagine him breaking down in the produce section of a grocery store somewhere, his body limp in my arms as I carry him back to some dark apartment where we'd live by ourselves. It's hard to be optimistic when you know you'll be on your own, when you know it will be only you in the D-Pediatric, waiting to hear whether your son will ever seem like a child again.

At the park we cross the fresh-mowed lawn. The sun cuts over a line of oleanders. A Mexican family is barbecuing flank steak under a picnic stand, and the smell fills the air. Cole's hand has improved enough for him to play catch, so we take our usual positions near the snack bar.

"So, Dad," he says, winding up like a big league pitcher, "you think I'll be able to play Little League next year?" He stares an imaginary runner back to first, then steps off the mound.

"You'll be eligible," I say. "You can try it if you want to."

He winds up again and throws a pitch that skids on the ground. "Sorry about that."

"Your arm all right?"

"Little sore," he says, and takes his mitt off and massages the shoulder. Even from twenty feet I can see the hand is twitching. "I'm trying to decide if it would be too much to do baseball *and* soccer," he says, and puts the mitt back on.

"What are Tanner and Sean going to do?" I ask.

"Tanner's gonna do both. Sean hasn't decided yet."

"Maybe you should just play baseball and see how it goes." I throw him a grounder, and he fields it and makes a pretend throw to first.

"Soccer's my main sport, though," he says with intensity. "I want to play soccer for sure." He throws a pitch that hits the grass just in front of him, then hustles up like a catcher going after a bunt. His throwing arm is shaking so badly he can't hold the ball, though, let alone make the throw, so he falls abruptly to a sitting position on the grass, pressing his bad hand into the mitt.

"You all right?" I ask.

"I just want to take a break," he says.

I walk over and sit down beside him.

Next to the covered picnic tables, a Mexican girl in a white lace dress takes swings at a piñata with a broomstick. Cole hunches over his mitt, rocking back and forth. It seems remarkable that he's been able to throw a ball at all, ever, that we've stood here and played catch and had it seem like a normal thing.

"Maybe we ought to go home," I say. "It's been a long day for everyone."

"I'll be all right in a second," he says.

I lean into him, touch his face. When he's looking at me, I say, "It's all right if you're having problems, you know. You don't have to hide anything from your dad."

"I'm not hiding," he says, but his eyes suddenly fill with desperation, and he has to glance off at the picnic tables, where the girl has broken the piñata and kids are clamoring underneath. He watches them, his jaw set tight. His voice, when he speaks, is thin and frightened. "What's going to happen, Dad?" he asks.

"You'll be fine," I say, because sometimes it's a father's job to lie. "Don't worry, Cole. You'll be great."

Don't
Call It
Christmas

When he got home that night it was raining hard and the girl lay in the entryway, crying. The boy was gone, but his chrome bike still stood against the wall. The girl glanced up from her dirty yellow blanket, eyes red, cheeks dark with mascara.

"What do you want?" she asked.

"I don't want anything," he said. "What happened to your friend?"

"How should I know?"

"You need any help?"

She shook her head.

He felt awkward, standing above her with his bag of Chinese food. It was the first time he'd spoken to the girl. The boy, with his phony accent, had always done the talking for both of them.

"Well, you can call me from right here if you need anything," he said, and waited until she looked at him. "I live in 2B."

She nodded, and he opened the front door. The rain was cold and blowing in from the street.

At the top of the landing he heard the phone ring, and at first he thought it might be the girl calling to ask for help. He quickly unlocked the door and set his food on the table. But it was only Erroll calling from the hospital in Phoenix.

"I hope I didn't catch you at a bad time," Erroll said, his voice bright and desperate.

"I just got home with some dinner," he said.

"I won't keep you, then," Erroll said. "I just wanted to let you know we had a hopeful week, is all. Your mother's GCS numbers are looking better, and her eyelids are fluttering like crazy. I keep expecting her to open her eyes and start chattering like a magpie!" He laughed his big laugh.

"That's great," Will said, though he knew it didn't mean anything at all. Erroll was always hopeful when he phoned.

"We'll show those doctors what the final verdict is," Erroll said.

"I hope so," Will said.

"So how you doing, kid? You able to get some work done?"

"I got a little done today."

"That's great. Anyway, I just wanted to let you know we had a good week. I'm betting on a merry Christmas. I just miss her so much, you know what I mean? I miss having her come home with some new cactus or a video she's read about in the papers — even if it's Japanese!"

"I know what you mean," Will said.

"I was alone for a long time before I met your mother."

"I know."

"Well, I'm going to let you eat your dinner now. I won't go on and on like an old man."

Will tried to think of something encouraging to say but

couldn't. He said, "Thanks for calling, Erroll. Let me know if anything changes."

"Oh, it changes all the time," Erroll said in his upbeat voice. "I'll keep you posted."

Will hung up the phone.

He went into the kitchen and opened a bottle of wine, then sat and poured a glass and looked out the window. Rain was coming down in sheets. The wine smelled of oak, and he drank it and looked at the people in the apartments across the courtyard: the Indian family on their long white couch, the husband reading to their blind little girl; the old Italian man working on one of his model ships. Will pictured his mother in a hospital bed with the tube in her nose. It pained him to imagine her like that. He had left Arizona when they'd told him nothing would change, and now every time he thought of her he pictured her with that tube. He took a sip of wine and felt his scalp tighten. As he filled his glass again, a light came on in the waitress's apartment. He stood and turned off the kitchen light.

The waitress walked through her apartment and into the kitchen, a pretty woman with thin white arms. He'd seen her in Katia's Restaurant on Haight Street, where she'd been his waitress once. She'd smiled and been friendly, but only in the way of waitresses. Now she stood in front of the refrigerator, drinking a can of soda. He watched her drink it quickly, then set the can on a counter and walk down the hall. A moment later she hurried through the apartment with a handbag over her shoulder. She went through the front door and left it ajar. He thought she'd return, but several minutes passed and she didn't.

The smell of Kung Pao chicken reminded him how hungry he'd been. He thought of the girl in the vestibule, sitting on the wet tiles. Maybe the boy was back now. The boy's name was Ian, and he and the girl had slept in the vestibule for a week, since the rains began. It was enough time for Will to wonder where they'd come from and how they managed to eat. If he were a different kind of person he would go downstairs and ask the girl up for some Chinese food, he thought, and then the idea of not being that kind of person made him angry. "I can do whatever I want," he said, standing. His voice sounded hollow in the empty apartment.

In the hallway he smelled sautéed onions and heard Nat King Cole's "A Christmas Song" coming from the floor above. He walked down the stairs to a place where he could crouch and see the entryway. The girl was there. She stared at the opposite wall of the vestibule, a blank expression on her face. She'd looked at him in just that way as he talked to Ian a few times, and Will had thought she either liked him or disliked him very much. He'd toyed with the idea of asking them both up to his apartment but had wondered what they'd do once they were in his little living room. Now he went down the stairs and crossed the tiled entryway. He opened the door to the sound of rain.

"You want to come up and have some Chinese food?" he asked.

The girl squinted up at him, her face round and white.

"I've got a bunch of Chinese food," he said. "I thought you might be hungry."

"No thanks."

"You sure? You could come up and get dry and eat something."

She gave him that hard-to-read expression, staring at him as if he were a wall or a statue. The earthly smell of her hair rose to him, along with the smell of the tiles.

"All right," she said. "I'll come."

"Great," he said, and held out a hand, his pulse beating in the back of his throat.

In his apartment she walked across the living room to the back window and laid her things on the floor. There was the dirty blanket and a backpack and a leather jacket with the word CRUX on the back. She wore rolled-up jeans, work boots, and a stained white T-shirt. Her hair, choppy and short, had been dyed the color of barbecue sauce.

"Pretty cool place," she said, looking around.

She was the first person he'd had in the apartment, and her presence seemed to change it, as if everything she looked at became real for the first time — the futon couch and the faded Navajo rug, the posters he'd taped to the walls. She picked up a candle from the coffee table, and it made his fingertips tingle. Just then the phone rang, and he took it into the bedroom. It was Father Abernathy calling from the high school.

"So how're you settling in?" the priest asked.

"Pretty good." Will glanced through the bedroom door. The girl had gone to the window and was looking out at the courtyard.

"Just wanted to see if you'd received the materials we sent," the priest said. "We want to be sure you're ready to roll come January."

"I've been going over the syllabus," Will said. "Father Dauphin's notes are pretty meticulous."

"He's a meticulous man," the priest said, "and one of the best educators we've ever had."

Three weeks earlier, Father Dauphin had tried to hang himself in a restroom stall at Saint Ignatius High School, where he'd taught freshman and sophomore English. He'd ended up bruising his trachea and was on medical leave. Will would take over his classes after the holidays. He'd gotten the job through a school in Tempe, where he'd been an assistant teacher for a few years after college.

"I spoke with him just this morning," the priest said. "He seemed in good spirits, given the circumstances. The trachea's healing nicely. They say sometimes the attempt is enough to take the impulse away. You really want to believe that."

"Sure," Will said.

"Well, I've got a Mass to give, but I'll call you after Christmas, how's that sound? We can discuss classes and any changes you might want to make."

Will thanked him and said good-bye.

When he came back to the living room, the girl was at the window. Across the courtyard, the waitress stood in front of a full-length mirror, wearing only a black skirt and a pale yellow bra. She took a blouse out of the closet.

The girl turned, her eyes thin and sharp, as if she'd been considering Will's view of the woman's apartment. He went into the kitchen and got his glass of wine.

"You want anything to drink?" he asked as he came back out.

"I'll have a beer, if you've got one," she said.

"How old are you?" he asked.

"Twenty-two."

"I don't believe you're *that* old," he said.

"Nineteen," she said, and gave him a challenging look.

She couldn't have been more than eighteen. It seemed wrong not to give her a beer, though, since he'd seen her drinking on Haight Street so many times, leaning against Quicker Liquor with Ian and their friends, hassling people for change. He got her a beer, and the two of them stood and drank as the rain beat against the window.

"I'm probably an alcoholic," she said, forking up a bite of Kung Pao chicken, staring at him in her odd, frank way. "I drink three forty-ouncers a night."

"Why?"

"How do I know why? I like getting wasted."

"You can't do it all the time, though," he said.

"Who says?"

"I don't know." He'd been taking in the details of her body — the dark roots of her hair, a slightly grayed front tooth that was chipped at the corner, a tattooed snake that coiled around her wrist like a bracelet.

"Why are you on the street?" he asked. "You run away or something?"

"Why would I tell you?"

"I guess you wouldn't. It's none of my business."

"My stepdad's an asshole," she said, and gave him a quick look before glancing out the window. The waitress was in her uniform now, moving through the apartment. She had on the white, puff-sleeved blouse she wore to the Russian restaurant where she worked.

"She's got a pretty neck," the girl said, touching her own. "It's long and thin. You like her, I bet. She looks like your type. She's pretty, but she doesn't look like a ho-bag or anything."

"Is that my type?" He laughed.

"How do I know?"

Will told her about the other people across the courtyard —

the Indian family and the old man who made model ships and the young couple whose blinds were always drawn. He told her about Boo Radley, who lived just below him. Will had never seen the man, but he'd heard him moving furniture around late at night and shouting strange things over and over.

"Not that you're a snoop," she said.

"Oh, I am, though," he said. "I've got so much time on my hands."

He told her he had no friends in town and had come to the city to teach the English classes of a priest who had tried to kill himself and that his mother was in a coma in Phoenix. It felt good to be saying these things.

"What happened to your mom?"

"She was in an accident. An old guy ran into her car on the highway. She had a head injury that didn't seem so bad at first, but then she just slipped into a coma."

"Why aren't you there?"

"I have to prepare for my classes, for one thing. This guy Erroll's there, her boyfriend. I guess I just didn't like seeing her with this — she had this tube in her nose, you know those things? She's been there for three months, and they don't think she'll come out of it. I don't see any reason to kid myself about it."

"Did you get along with her?" she asked.

"Yeah. We were close."

Across the way the waitress's lights went out. A lamp flickered in the courtyard.

"I'm from Phoenix, too," she said. "I went to Arcadia for two years."

"No kidding? I went to Saguaro. My girlfriend went to Arcadia. My ex-girlfriend, that is. That's another thing — my girlfriend broke up with me." He laughed, as if it were a joke he'd told.

"Nice life," she said.

"Tell me about it."

After dinner, he said he'd go to the Video Den to rent a movie. She could stay and watch if she wanted to. She thought about it, biting her lip, and finally said, "All right, but I can't go with you. My friends'd freak if they saw me with you."

He went down Page Street in a light rain and rented a movie from the Albanian clerk. Coming out, he saw the girl's friends in front of the liquor store, drinking beers from paper sacks. Ian wasn't among them, but Will recognized the others — a boy with a chamois-colored mohawk, a heavyset Latina girl. It was a thrill to see them and know the girl was in his apartment. A couple of them were burning papers on the sidewalk, tossing in band flyers and cigarette packs, laughing.

The girl was on the couch when he got home, sipping a beer, watching MTV. He went to the kitchen and saw that she'd washed the dishes and stacked them in the rack.

"Thanks for cleaning up," he said.

"That's all right. I'm pretty clean, actually."

She smelled of wet leather, though she'd taken her jacket off. He sat down beside her.

The movie, *Sid and Nancy*, was one she'd requested. In it, all the characters spoke in cockney accents like Ian, dropping their h's, telling each other to bugger off. The girl had seen it once, but she watched it carefully, as if secrets were being revealed. Will got caught up in it, too, because it was a good movie, better than he'd expected. For nearly two hours, with the TV flashing and the story playing out on the screen, he forgot about the girl beside him and his ex-girlfriend and his mother. Then the movie was over and his life took its old form around him. Boo Radley shouted in the apartment below. Will stood and turned on the overhead light.

"What's that?" the girl asked, listening to Boo.

"That weird guy I told you about."

The man's voice came through the floorboards. "The situation is the predicament! The situation stinks!"

"That's weird," she said.

"I hardly even notice him anymore."

"It stinks!" the man shouted. "It's unacceptable!"

They listened for a moment, but the man had quieted down.

"Hey, if you wanna crash on the couch you can," Will said. He'd almost asked her earlier but had feared she might take it the wrong way. Now it had just come out.

"All right," she said.

"Great," he said, surprised at how easy it had been.

As he washed his face and brushed his teeth, he was pleased that the girl would be in the apartment while he tried to sleep. He'd had trouble sleeping lately. Sometimes he'd wake in the middle of the night with his heart pounding like a hammer in his chest. When he did sleep, he'd dream of his mother waking in her hospital bed, pulling that tube out of her nose. It would be nice to have someone in the apartment if he woke up from a dream like that. He found a pillow and blanket in the linen closet and brought them out to the living room.

"I've already got a blanket," the girl said, nodding at the filthy one she'd spread on the futon.

"I'll just leave this in case it gets cold," he said.

"All right. Hey, thanks for letting me crash. My name's Amity, by the way."

"I'm Will." He leaned over and shook her hand, an awkward gesture after their evening together. Her hand was smooth and warm, and it gave him a charge to touch it. In bed, he thought of her for a long time before he fell asleep.

In the morning she was at the kitchen table, flipping through a magazine. She wore the jeans and dirty white T-shirt she'd worn the day before.

"You sleep all right?" he asked.

"I slept great," she said.

He said he had to go to the library and get some work done but that she could stay if she wanted. She said she might.

He gathered some quarters so she could wash her clothes in the laundry room and gave her sweatpants and a T-shirt to wear. Then he went to the library and worked hard for several hours, reading Father Dauphin's xeroxed notes. They were written in the priest's tiny, meticulous hand, the letters small and precise as ants. As he read them, Will tried not to think of the man swinging from the crossbar of a restroom stall. Occasionally he'd remember Amity and hope she'd be in the apartment when he got home, but he didn't think she would be. The last six months had taught him to be pessimistic. He still felt the buzz from his time with her, though. Lately he'd gone whole days without talking to anyone except the woman at the Chinese restaurant, who never seemed to understand what he said anyway.

He walked home in a light rain. Outside the post office a gray-haired woman stood ringing a Salvation Army bell, the collar of her coat turned up against the cold. He thought of his mother in her yellow work jacket, a hardhat pushed back on her head. After his father had died, Will's mother had talked his bosses into taking her on at the Salt River Project where he'd worked. Every morning she'd gone out with a crew of linesmen and repaired power cables and utility closets. She'd come home at night and make dinner and eat with Will. She loved to laugh. He always tried to remember jokes because a good one would make her throw her head back and howl. She liked it when he brought friends home from school, and she would talk to them as if they were her own friends. Somehow she managed to pay the bills and save enough money for his college tuition. She'd always been stubborn and independent, which made it hard to think of her in the hospital, where machines were keeping her alive.

On Haight Street, wreaths in the shape of peace signs hung from all the light poles. Will went into a pizzeria and ordered a large pie with sausage and pepperoni. As he stepped out he saw Amity's friends near the head shop across the street. Ian was there, pedaling his little chrome bike around. He saw Will and rode over, popping the bike onto the sidewalk.

"Ey, Wil-li-am," he said in his phony accent. He was a good-looking kid with bright blue eyes and hair that stood up from his scalp like quills.

"How you doing, Ian?"

"I feel right dodgy, if you want to know," Ian said. "I lost me bird last night."

"What bird?" Will asked.

"Me *bird*," he said. "Am-i-ty. You 'aven't seen 'er, 'ave you?"

"Not for a couple days," Will said.

Ian glanced across the street. Two kids stood in front of the laundromat — a thin Latino and a heavyset girl whose eyes were painted like a raccoon's. They'd been watching Ian. He shook his head at them, and they turned and walked west on Haight Street.

"I'm out of me 'ead about this," Ian said to Will.

"When's the last time you saw her?"

"Last night. We was kipping out front of your gaff, right? Then off I go to have a whizzer, and two minutes later come back and she's gone. We think she might of got nipped by the cops."

"Well, I'll let you know if I see her," Will said. He started down the sidewalk and was half a block away when Ian called his name. He turned around.

"You 'aving a pizza, then?" Ian called.

"Yeah. Why?"

"Awfully big pie for one bloke, innit?"

"Not really." Will felt his throat tighten like a fist.

Ian leaned forward, his eyes sharp and narrow. Then his face broke into an enormous grin and he said, "Aw, give us a slice, will ya! Don't be so bleedin' stingy!"

When he got home, Amity was on the living-room floor, her things laid out before her: piles of clean clothes and stacks of magazines, cassette tapes, Sterno cans, pistachio nuts, coins, cans of hair spray. She had on the maroon sweatpants and T-shirt he'd given her to wear. Her hair was shiny and flat.

"You look different," he said.

"I'm all organized," she said, gazing proudly over her possessions. "I've needed to do this for weeks."

He laid the pizza on the kitchen table, and they ate and watched the Italian man build his ships on the other side of the courtyard. At first, Will couldn't stop thinking about Ian — picturing him on the little chrome bicycle, riding up and down Haight Street, searching for Amity. But watching the old man was soothing, and after a while he was able to put Ian out of his mind. The old man glued strips of balsa wood to a sleek, double-masted schooner. On a shelf behind him were all the ships he'd made — galleons and clippers, all with intricate riggings and sails. The rain gave the scene the hazy look of an old daguerreotype.

As they finished their pizza, the waitress came home and Amity got up and turned off the light. They watched the woman put her things away and change into her uniform. Her pale shoulders showed for a moment, but that was all. After she'd dressed, she ate a few bites of ice cream from a carton, standing in front of the freezer, then smoked a cigarette and went out again. The man downstairs began to holler.

"That guy likes her," Amity said. "He goes off every time she leaves the apartment."

"I never noticed that before."

"I heard him all day long," she said. "He's like a bird. He gets all excited for a while, then just gets quiet."

"What was he saying today?"

"He was saying, 'There are reasons for everything, causes and excuses.' He kept yelling that."

"He says that a lot. He also says, 'It was heretofore unrecognized' and 'Damn your rhetorical stance!'"

"He's a freak. What did you say his name was again?"

"Boo Radley. But it's not his real name." Will went into the living room and took *To Kill a Mockingbird* from his bookshelf. "It's the name of a character in this book. You ever read it?"

She took the book and studied its cover.

"You should read it," he said. "You'd like it, I bet."

"Maybe," she said.

She washed the dishes while he went to the Video Den and rented one of his favorites, a Sri Lankan film about three boys who dive for lobsters during World War II. He was anxious as he watched it, hoping she'd like it, too. A bag of microwave popcorn stood between them. After the movie was over, she turned to him with a dazed look in her eyes.

"What's the matter?" he asked.

"That was the best movie I've ever seen," she said. "I didn't think I'd like it, but I totally did."

That night as he lay in bed he couldn't stop thinking of her. Maybe she would leave in the morning and it would be for the best, though it pained him to think of her going. For the first time in several weeks he drifted off without thinking about his mother.

The next day at the library, as he waded through Father Dauphin's notes on *Ethan Frome*, he felt like a detective uncovering clues. The margins were filled with notations like, *This book is about the Ascension!* and *This book has the Passion written all over it!* As far as Will could tell, the notations referred to nothing.

When he came home Amity was not on the couch or in the kitchen, though her things still lay on the floor by the window. He got a beer from the fridge and went into the bedroom. Amity lay there on the bed, sleeping, a copy of *To Kill a Mockingbird* on the pillow beside her. He tried to slip out of the room, but she woke and looked at him.

"I fell asleep in here," she said. "I hope that's all right."

"Of course it is."

"I read this book," she said, and held it up. "I read the whole thing in one day."

"Did you like it?"

"You crazy? It's about the best book I ever read," she said.

He sat down beside her. "I've got other ones you can read if you want."

"If they're as good as that one, I'll read them."

"Some you might like even better."

"I doubt it," she said. "But I'll check them out." She gave him her expressionless look, her eyes distant and blue. "You can kick me out anytime, though. I don't mind if you want me to go."

"I'm not going to kick you out. I like having you here."

"I've got to go sometime. It's not like I can stay forever. But I'm not saying I want to leave right away."

"That's good," he said, and smiled at her.

"What?"

"Nothing. You're sweet."

"Yeah, right," she said. "I'm not sweet."

"You are, though." He leaned over and kissed her on the lips. She smelled of toothpaste and clean laundry.

"What's that for?"

"Nothing," he said. "I like you."

"You're weird," she said.

"You are."

He kissed her again, and this time she put her hands around his back and pulled him toward her. For a few seconds the room seemed to tip and recede.

They made love with the rain ticking against the window. Boo Radley shouted in the apartment below, insisting that there were reasons for everything, causes and excuses. A light-headed feeling came over Will, so that for a moment he felt he was rising into the air like vapor. Amity's eyes were closed; she was breathing quickly. Soon it was over, and he felt dazed and frightened. Amity lay facing the wall.

"You all right?" he asked, but she only moved a little farther away from him.

"Don't talk to me now," she said.

He watched the raindrops roll down the window glass. The sky outside seemed to brighten and dim, as if someone were turning a knob. "I sure hope you're all right, though," he said.

She began to cry, her shoulders bucking. He put a hand on her arm, but she shrugged it away. After a moment, she sat up and looked straight ahead into the room.

"I'm all right," she said. "Forget I cried, okay?"

"Okay," he said, but he didn't think he would.

———

The next morning, he let her sleep while he had breakfast and prepared for work. He went into the bedroom before leaving, and she was sitting up. She said, "Good morning," but gave no indication of how she felt about the night before.

As he walked to the library, he saw Ian coming up Shrader, mumbling a song to himself, holding a little spray-painted radio under his arm. Ian saw Will and called out "Hey!" and staggered up the street. He'd had the word KILLED tattooed on his forehead — the letters in black, each an inch or so high. Ian grinned, touching them with his fingertips.

"That's the extra 'eavy 'piss off' special," he said, "which I sold me bleedin' bike to get."

"Pretty serious," Will said.

"I'm in it to the grave now, mate."

"I guess you are," Will said. "Hey, did you ever find Amity?"

"Yeah, she came back last night. It was the cops, the tossers. Actually, we 'ad a fight and I told 'er to piss off, so she's gone back wiff 'er mum in Arizona. She was taking the piss out of me, you know what I'm saying?"

"Is that where you're from, too? Arizona?"

"You fucking daft? I'm from Liverpool, ya cunt. Hey, give us a few quid, will ya? I'm starving."

Will took out his wallet. He couldn't stop glancing at the tattoo, which was dark and horrible against Ian's forehead. "I don't have any quid. This is America, remember?" He gave Ian a few bucks, and Ian kissed them and stuffed them into his pocket.

"Hey, you remember that cap I use to wear?" he said. "Biker cap, like? Leather? I lost it." He seemed suddenly worried. "I got no bleedin' idea where it went. It was sort of me personality, you know, that cap. You ever have something like that?"

"I don't think I have," Will said.

"It was German," Ian said. His accent had faded. "Anyway, fuck it." He tried to grin at Will, then gave up and walked west toward Golden Gate Park. "See you when I see you," he called.

"Not if I see you first," Will said under his breath.

He tried to concentrate on Father Dauphin's notes but couldn't stop thinking about Ian and Amity. He remembered a dream his girlfriend Darcy had in his room one night, a few months before he left for San Francisco. It was the night she'd told him she was seeing a man named Robert French, whom she'd met playing golf at her father's country club. French was a forty-year-old corporate lawyer with a wife and three young boys. She'd been out with him three times and was in love with him, she said. She and Will talked about it for several hours, then she fell asleep while he lay listening to the ambulances on their way to Saint Luke's Hospital.

In the dream, Jesus came to Darcy on the golf course where she'd met French, riding a little gold-plated golf cart, His white robe blowing back over the club rack. Darcy was frightened, but

Jesus only stepped off of the cart and said, "Please, Darcy, you've done nothing wrong." He spread his arms wide and smiled beatifically. "All of human life is a tie," he said. "Charlie Manson ties with Helen Keller. Adolf Hitler ties with Mother Teresa. We all do the best we can given the circumstances."

Darcy had laughed, telling Will the dream in the morning, and he'd hated her for it — hated her finding humor in something so devastating to him, for finding comfort in a dream so opposed to his beliefs. Now he imagined Darcy and Christ, holding hands, drifting down from the high library ceiling, watching him with benign, self-satisfied eyes.

When he came home he was relieved to find Amity at the kitchen table, staring at the lighted windows across the courtyard. The Indian family were decorating a Christmas tree in their living room, the father placing orange balls in the blind daughter's hands, leading her to the tree so she could hang them on the low branches.

"It's a pretty tree," he said, and sat down beside Amity. He wanted to catch her eye, but she wouldn't turn from the window. "They're almost finished, huh?"

"I've been watching them all day," she said in a quiet voice. "I feel almost like I've been doing it with them."

The mother unraveled garland from a piece of cardboard. She wore a bright red sari that seemed a part of the decoration.

"The old guy's got one, too," she said, pointing at the apartment below.

On the Italian man's desk stood a tiny fir, a few paper ornaments hanging from its branches.

"That's kind of a sad one," he said.

"I thought so at first," she said, "but it's not. He just wanted a tree. What's wrong with that?"

"I suppose you're right."

"I was thinking we should get one, too. Just a small one like that."

He tried not to appear excited. "Sounds like a good idea," he said, and went to the fridge for a beer. On the counter was a bag of pot and a silver-and-turquoise lighter.

"Where did this stuff come from?" he asked.

"My friend Kathy."

"You went out?"

"So what?" she said.

"Nothing," he said. "How did you get back in, though?"

"Put a newspaper in the door."

"What about your friends? I thought you didn't want anyone to know you were here."

"I only told Kathy. Kathy won't narc on me."

"You must get tired of being stuck up here all day," he said.

"It's not so bad." She nodded at the apartments across the courtyard. "I was thinking we should get presents for those people over there. For the man and the family and the waitress lady. We could write 'From Santa Claus' or something and put them by their doors. Then we'd knock and come back and watch everyone open their presents."

"We could do that," he said, suddenly elated. He thought: I'll take what comes my way. I won't try to stop it from happening.

"I already know what I want to get for everybody," Amity said.

"All right. We can go shopping after I work tomorrow."

"You think we can get ornaments like those people's over there?"

"Why not?"

"We'll make some, too," she said, "to save money. Like with popcorn and string."

"We'll use microwave popcorn," he said. "We've already got that."

"Right," she said. "And we'll get totally wasted."

He laughed. "Maybe we'll get a little wasted. I can teach you some drinking games I learned in college."

She narrowed her eyes, almost as if she were angry. "I'll totally fuck you up."

───────────

It rained hard the next day. Will went to the library and tried to work but could only think of Amity and how they would decorate the tree. He'd come to believe he'd have no Christmas at all that year and had convinced himself it didn't matter, but now that he had plans he knew how much he would have missed it. He sat watching a librarian read to a group of children in the corner of the library, her voice bright and round. The room was hot. He laid his head on the table and drifted off to sleep.

When he woke, the light in the high windows was dim. He went out into the iron-smelling rain and up to Haight Street, where he bought a couple of burritos and horchatas at El Balazo. Coming out, he saw Ian on the sidewalk, shirtless under a leather jacket, his hair wet and hanging in his face. Ian took two steps and slapped Will's bag of food out of his hands.

"What's that for?" Will asked, but he could see in Ian's eyes what it was for.

"I know she's up there," Ian said, his accent gone. "I know what's going on."

"What are you talking about?"

"Cut it out, man. I mean it. I need money from you now. I need a hundred and forty bucks."

"What for?" Will asked.

"Don't ask questions," Ian said. He started down Haight Street, turning to shoot Will a threatening look. "Let's go, fucker."

Will followed him. They passed the bookstore and the pizzeria. People walked past them with umbrellas angled at the rain. A police cruiser crossed Haight at Cole Street and disappeared around the corner.

"I can't give you money," Will said. "I barely have any in my account right now."

"Bullshit," Ian said, and kept walking.

"I mean it, Ian."

Ian swung around. "Do you know what this is?" he asked, opening his jacket. The handle of a buck knife stuck out of his waistband, the metal rusted to a reddish brown.

At the ATM, they waited behind a man in a clear plastic rain jacket. Will hoped the man would see the knife and go for help, but he only took his money and walked away. Will thought of Amity lying in his bed in the apartment. A few people went past, their eyes on the wet sidewalk.

"What do you need the money for?" Will asked.

"Don't worry about it. I owe a guy."

"What for?"

"None of your fucking business."

"I won't give it to you unless you tell me," Will said. He felt like he ought to take a stand on something.

"You want me to fucking stab you?"

"I don't think you'll stab me," Will said.

Ian let out a barking laugh. "What's the matter with you, man? You think you can do whatever you want and get away with it? She's my *girlfriend*, man. Don't you get that? She's fucking *seventeen*."

"I didn't know that," Will said. "I'm sorry it happened."

"You're gonna make me puke," Ian said. He bent over and spat on the sidewalk, looking for a moment as if he really might get sick. People had come up behind him to use the machine.

Will took out his wallet and said, "Look, I'll get the money from my credit account, just stand up, all right?"

Ian stood and turned to the people behind him, shaking his head. "Old dude with a homeless chick," he said. "Makes you wanna puke."

When he got home that night the phone was ringing, and he picked it up and took it into the kitchen. It was Erroll on the line. The tone of his voice made Will's heart beat fast.

"I hope you're sitting down, kid," Erroll said.

"Why?" Will said. "What happened?"

"She's come out of it," Erroll said.

Will glanced at the courtyard. The rain was slanting through a strip of light. "When?" he asked.

"This morning, around eleven. Your mother's awake."

Amity came in and gave him a searching look. He shook his head. "You're kidding me," he said into the phone.

"I wouldn't kid you about this one," Erroll said, laughing. "It just happened a few hours ago."

"So — can she talk and everything? Is she conscious? Does she know what happened?" He leaned against the wall and thought of his mother glancing up from the hospital bed, her eyes wide and alert. He couldn't make himself believe it.

"Well, that takes time, I guess. But she's come out of it now, and the doctors are excited. This is the big one, kid."

"This is crazy," Will said.

Erroll laughed. "I can hardly believe it myself. Listen, kid, I'm in the coffee shop. I don't want to miss the doctor when he returns. I'll call you from the room, okay? Don't get *too* excited."

"No, I'll try not to," Will said, and hung up the phone.

"Was that about your mom?" Amity asked. She was wearing his maroon ASU shirt. Her eyes were wide.

"Erroll says she came out of her coma. He was just calling from the hospital."

"Holy shit," she said.

He had to sit at the table. His heart was racing.

"What are you gonna do?" she asked.

"I don't know. Go home." He shook his head. "I can't believe this is happening."

"It's pretty fucking amazing."

"I'll probably leave tomorrow," he said. "You can come with me if you want."

She seemed to consider it.

Something was wrong, he thought. He didn't deserve good news, because he'd acted inappropriately. That was why it was hard to believe his mother was awake. And yet Erroll had just told him she was awake. He thought of Ian, and a wave of guilt moved through him. He knew he'd have to tell Amity about Ian.

"When would we decorate the tree?" she asked.

"We could still do it tonight, I guess."

"I want to give those people their presents," she said.

"We'd get back in time. I still have to come back and get ready to teach."

"Could you take me to see my mom when we're in Phoenix?"

"Of course," he said.

"All right," she said, and bit a thumbnail. "I guess I've got nothing better to do."

He woke the next morning to the sound of hail against the window. It was light out, nine o'clock. Amity was sleeping. He kissed her cheek and went out to the kitchen, where their little tree stood on the table. It was covered with lights and popcorn strings. They'd spent all night decorating it. He'd tried several times to tell her about Ian but couldn't make himself do it. He didn't want to take her out of their time together.

Across the courtyard the waitress stood at her window, wearing a terry-cloth robe, staring at the hail. She saw Will and waved in a friendly way, as if they were the kind of neighbors who waved each morning.

He went downstairs to get the paper. The girl with raccoon eyes sat in the entryway, slumped against the wall, a sleeping bag draped around her shoulders. The hail danced in the street behind her.

"Morning," he said, but she only glared at him, so he went back inside.

Upstairs, Amity was awake and talking on the phone, dressed in jeans and an old white tank top. "I'll come down," she said, and hung up.

"Who was that?" he asked.

"Kathy."

"Nothing's wrong, is it?"

"How should I know? I'm going down and talk to her. Did you know it's hailing outside?"

"I saw that," he said.

"That waitress was looking out the window," she said. "She waved at me."

"She waved at me, too," he said.

Amity put on her leather jacket and went out the door.

He poured a bowl of cornflakes and tried to read the paper. Downstairs Boo Radley was chanting too softly to be understood. Amity came in a few minutes later, out of breath, looking him hard in the eye. He felt the cold air coming off her.

"You gave him money," she said.

"Who?"

"Don't be stupid," she said. "You know who. Why would you give him money?"

"He's all right, isn't he?"

"No, he's not all right. He's in Arizona. He bought a bus ticket with the money you gave him. He went home."

Will let out the breath he'd been holding. "I thought you were going to tell me he'd OD'd or something."

She walked over and swept his bowl off the table. It clattered across the linoleum floor.

"What was I supposed to do? He said he needed the money."

"That's bullshit," she said. "Anyway, you should have told me about it."

"I was going to, but then Erroll called and everything got crazy."

"It's too late now," she said.

"Are you thinking of going after him?"

"Of course I am. He's my boyfriend."

"I didn't know you thought of him that way," Will said.

"Well, now you know."

He looked out at the hailstones that salted the courtyard. It had started raining. Across the way the Indian family's Christmas tree was lighted, and they sat beside it on the sofa.

"What about us?" he said.

"It was a mistake," she said.

"You think so?"

"I consider it a kind of rape, even," she said, holding his gaze.

"Well, if you're only seventeen, it was," he said. "I sure didn't think of it that way, though. I didn't think you did, either."

She took her leather jacket off and started picking through the clothes on the floor. She found her T-shirt, then bunched the hem of Will's shirt and pulled it off. The sight of her small breasts in the gray light from the window was one of the saddest things he'd ever seen. She put her own shirt on and began to stuff clothes into her backpack.

"I sure wish you wouldn't leave," he said.

She stuffed everything into the pack — clothes, cassette tapes, pistachio nuts. When she'd finished, she swung the pack over her shoulder and went through the front door. Will heard her footsteps in the hall. In a minute, a loud thump rattled his window, and he walked out and saw her halfway to the bottom of the stairs, belly down, her things scattered on the landing below her.

"You all right?" he asked.

"Go away," she said, lifting herself with her arms. She gathered her things quickly and hurried down the stairs.

He went back to the apartment. The T-shirt she'd worn was on the floor. He picked it up and breathed in the smell of her skin. She'd left a can of hair spray, some magazines, the dirty yellow blanket she'd had the first day she came to the apartment. In the bedroom he threw the shirt in the laundry, then got a suitcase out of the closet and started to pack.

He found her on Haight Street, sitting under the Red Victorian ticket window, passing a cigarette back and forth with Kathy. The street was empty. He pulled in front of the theater and rolled down his window.

"I'm on my way to Phoenix," he called to her.

"So what?" she said, looking off at the tall trees in the park.

"I can take you to see Ian if you want. I'll bring you both back if he wants to come."

"His name's not even Ian," she said, and looked at him hatefully. "You're such a fucking idiot. You probably think he's from England."

Kathy snorted at that, flicking her cigarette into the street.

"I'm only trying to help," Will said.

"He went to your stupid high school," Amity said.

Will got out of the car and walked around the hood. "I'll take you to see him if you want," he said. "If not, that's fine. I just wanted to tell you I'm leaving."

She looked at him very carefully. She was sitting on her jacket, the sleeves of her T-shirt rolled up. He knew she was thinking so he went back to the car and let her talk to Kathy for a while. Finally, she stood and slung the backpack over her shoulder.

"I'm only going because I need to talk to Ian," she said. "Kathy's writing down your license plate number. If you try anything you're fucked."

For a brief moment, as she slid into the car beside him, he felt happy again. His mother, as far as he knew, was recovering in Phoenix, and he was going to see her with a girl he liked. It wasn't a feeling that could hold itself together, of course. He started the car and pulled away from the curb. In the rearview mirror Kathy grabbed her crotch and flipped him the bird.

"I like your friend," he said.

"Well, she hates you, too," Amity said. "Most people do, I bet."

"They probably do," he said.

There were no cars on the road, and he drove down Haight past the pizza place and the bookstore. Bars of light shone between the Victorian houses. Near Ashbury, Amity's friends were all out in the street, playing hackey sack.

"There they are," she said, straightening up in her seat.

The friends' mouths dropped open as Will passed them. He watched them in the rearview mirror, all of them gesturing at the car and shouting.

"Everyone knows what happened now," she said craning her head around. "They probably think I'm with you, which is hilarious. Maybe they'll set your house on fire."

"I almost hope they do," he said.

At Masonic he cut down two streets and drove along the panhandle, which lay under a blanket of fog. The two bell towers of Saint Ignatius stood above the gray.

"Did you see his tattoo?" she asked. "Kathy told me about it."

"Yeah, I saw it."

"He's such a fuckup," she said, smiling at the corners of her mouth.

He followed the signs to the Bay Bridge. The sky was steel gray, the water the color of tar. Amity took a copy of *The Catcher in the Rye* out of her coat pocket and opened it.

"I took this from your house," she said, and settled into reading as they drove past Oakland.

By the time they reached Barstow the sun was low and warm. Will stopped at a gas station with an enormous brontosaurus out front, the letters G-A-S painted across its apple-green belly. Amity got out and called Ian on the pay phone, curling the metal cord around her wrist. Will bought some sandwiches at the convenience store. When he came out she was walking back to the car.

"He's staying at Deke's," she said. "He's pissed at you. He's pissed at both of us, actually."

"So what are you going to do?" he asked.

"Who knows? Go home, I guess. I wouldn't mind staying with my mom for a while."

"What about your stepdad?"

"I don't really have one," she said, looking at the big dinosaur. "I don't know why I told you that."

They both got in the car.

"Gary has a stepdad," she said, musingly, as he pulled out of the lot. "I guess that's why I said that. Gary is Ian's real name, in case you're wondering." She shook her head in a solemn way. "His stepdad used to beat the living shit out of him."

It was dark by the time they neared Phoneix. Will could make out the round buttes rising like heads from the desert. He drove into the valley, past the botanical gardens and the Camelback Colonnade. Heading up Camelback Mountain, he followed Amity's directions and passed modern and Spanish-style homes set into the hill. He saw the starry blanket of Paradise Valley and the dark patch of desert beyond. Amity led him down a long private drive, at the end of which a villa lay spread out among palms and cacti.

"Nice place," Will said.

"Actually, my mom lives *there*," she said, and pointed to a long outbuilding with small windows. It stood a little down the hill from the villa. "I wasn't going to tell you," she said.

The building looked to have been a horse stable at one time. The wood had faded to a silver gray. Through one of the windows, Will saw a fridge and a strip of avocado wallpaper.

"She must have a good view of the valley," he said.

"She cooks for the guy who owns the place."

Will looked up at the big house. A strand of white Christmas lights wound around two ocotillos in the front yard.

Back at the stable building, a light went on, then a woman's face came into the window.

"There's Mom," Amity said, and raised a hand.

The woman stared for a moment, then waved.

"When's the last time you were here?" he asked.

"Couple of months ago. I haven't lived here for over a year, though."

"You don't get along with your mom?"

"Not really. Why? Do you?"

"I always have."

"That's right," she said. "You told me that. You must be psyched she woke up."

"I am," he said, and it was true. He'd nearly forgotten to feel good about it.

A door opened, and Amity's mother stepped onto a wooden porch. She was small and wore denim pants and a blue tank top.

"What's she doing?" Amity asked. "Go inside, Mom. She probably wants to meet you or something."

"I'd meet her."

"Yeah, right," she said. "Actually, I wanted to ask if you'd take me to see Gary tomorrow. Otherwise I don't know how I'll get there."

"I'll take you." He knew he'd do anything to see her again, even take her to see Ian — or Gary.

"Just if you have time," she said. "You can come whenever."

"I'll come," he said. "I'll see you tomorrow."

She got out of the car. He watched her sling her pack over her shoulder and walk up the drive. Her mother was smiling, tucking a loose strand of hair behind her ear. Before he pulled away, Amity turned and squinted into his headlights, and he waved, but he was sure she couldn't see him.

He arrived at the hospital long past visiting hours, but no one stopped him as he walked through the empty lobby. On the third floor he simply went into the room where his mother had been before, and she was there — lying on one of the beds, the machines around her, the tube in her nose. The other bed was empty. Erroll slept in a chair by the window.

He went to her bed and looked at her face, which was paler than it had been before. He lifted her hand and pressed the nail bed of her thumb, as he'd seen the doctors do. There was no response.

He touched her cheek—nothing. Then he sat on the bed and listened to the respirator breathing in and out. It wasn't her, he could see that—no more than it had been her before he left. He'd only allowed himself to half believe it would be. But the part of him that had believed it was reeling.

He went to the window. Two security guards stood under a fluorescent light in the parking lot, their hands in their pockets. A car's headlights went on. A noise came from behind Will, and he turned and saw Erroll sitting up in his chair. Erroll's face brightened for a moment before collapsing. He tried to stand but couldn't seem to get out of the chair. "She slipped back in," he said.

"I saw that," Will said.

"She just—" Erroll turned his eyes up, concentrating. "They really don't know what happened yet. I'm so sorry about it, Will."

A dull anger rose in Will's chest, but it faded quickly.

"I tried to call you," Erroll said. "I hated to think of you driving out here in the dark all alone."

"It's all right."

"It's still a good sign that it happened. I know you might not want to hear that right now."

"I'd like to hear everything, eventually," Will said.

"You're probably exhausted," Erroll said.

"I'm all right."

"Did you eat yet?"

"I stopped along the way."

"The cafeteria's closed, but there's vending machines down the hall."

Will went over and sat on the edge of the empty bed. He let his body fall back against the mattress.

"You can sleep there if you want," Erroll said. "They don't mind. I've done it myself a few times."

Will didn't think he'd sleep. He listened to the hum of the machines, thinking about Amity, thinking about what his life would be like once he returned to San Francisco. He'd have to prepare for the classes, which he didn't want to do. He decided that as soon as he got home he'd gather Father Dauphin's notes and burn them in the sink, and that made him feel better. He'd have to think of something to replace them with, of course. He heard a siren somewhere on the streets, below, a distant peal. As the sound grew louder, he knew he could sleep. Before it reached the hospital he'd already drifted off.

When he woke the room was warm, and the sky through the window was a pale, cloudless blue. Erroll was talking to Will's mother, too quietly to be understood.

"I hope I didn't wake you," he said, when Will sat up in the bed.

"No, I woke up on my own," Will said.

"I feel like I have to keep talking to her. I think she'd miss it if I didn't."

The two of them went down to the cafeteria. Over scrambled eggs and toast Erroll gave Will the prognosis: his mother's score on the Glasgow Coma Scale had gone from a three to a seven, which meant her chances of waking were significantly improved. Will was doubtful at first, but in the room later an intern told him more or less the same thing, though he also said it was still unlikely that his mother would regain consciousness.

"I just wish you could have seen this place yesterday," Erroll said, after the intern had gone. He stood by Will's mother's bed, holding her hand. "Everybody running around, going crazy, your mother with her eyes open, taking it all in." He glanced at Will's mother's face as if she might look back at him at any moment.

Will parked in front of the old stable building and watched Amity come out the front door, dressed in a muscle shirt and red shorts, her legs pale, her hair clean and pulled back in barrettes. She got in beside him, and he drove between the palm trees that lined the drive. Everything looked different in the daylight — the flat sprawl of the valley, the shocking red of the desert. Saguaros dotted the hills.

She stared at him as they wound their way down Camelback. "So how was it seeing your mom?"

He told her what had happened. She seemed upset, and he liked her for that.

"So what will you do now?" she said.

"I might stay for a week or so. It'd be good to spend some time with Erroll."

"Man, that sucks, though," she said.

He followed her directions through Scottsdale. Everything was strange and familiar — the pink buttes and the cacti and the palo-verde trees. At the corner of Templeton and Willetta, he took a right and entered a treeless neighborhood of low cinderblock houses.

"You weren't supposed to turn there," she told him.

He pulled in front of a one-story ranch-style house with gravel in the yard. "That's the house I grew up in," he said.

She looked at the house, then at him.

"My mom killed a rattlesnake right there," he said, pointing to the spot in the yard where it had happened. He pictured his mother coming out of the house in Capri pants, her hair dyed the color of straw.

The girl looked into the yard as if there were something to see there.

Her friend lived in a beige house on a street called China Drive. An aluminum boat lay upside-down in the yard, and there were old car doors and fenders strewn here and there. Will saw a TV flashing through the screen door.

"I wouldn't mind talking to Ian," he said, as he pulled to the curb. "I don't like having him mad at me."

"I don't think he'll talk to you," she said. But she got out and walked up to the house to ask him. Will got out and leaned against the car door. He felt the heat on the crown of his head. In a few minutes Amity came out and crossed the lawn.

"He won't talk to you," she said. "He almost did, but Deke wouldn't let him."

"I appreciate your asking."

"He's still pretty pissed," she said. "I saw his tattoo, though. That shit is messed up."

"He's in it to the grave," Will said.

"Yeah, no doubt."

"So what will you do now? You going to stay in Arizona?"

"Yeah, I'll probably stay with my mom a while."

"You won't go back to San Francisco?"

"Nah. It was a hassle to get there. I thought it would be all sunny and a bunch of hippies and everything. But it's not. It's cold and depressing."

The screen door banged open and Ian emerged, shirtless, a skullcap pulled down over his forehead. He crossed the lawn. " 'Ello, Will-i-am," he called in his cockney accent.

"How's it going, Ian?"

He walked up behind Amity and grabbed her waist. Then he looked at Will and stopped smiling. "Hey, sorry about your mom, dude. Amity told me about it."

"It's a bad situation," Will said.

"No doubt." Ian glanced down the street. A woman stood in her yard two houses away, holding a hose over a row of dying hydrangeas. "So you went to Saguaro, huh?"

"That's right," Will said.

"Sabercats, dude," Ian said, and widened his eyes. " 'Neath the blazing sun of old Saguar-a-ro.' You remember singing that shit?"

"I do," Will said. "It's a long time ago, though."

"You musta graduated in the Stone Ages, huh?" Ian laughed and looked at Amity.

"Just about," Will said. "Eight years ago."

"Jesus, dude, you're so old! I hope I never get that old."

"Sadly," Will said, "it's the best you can hope for."

"Yeah, no kidding, huh?"

A wiry kid came out the door and glared at Will. He wore denim cutoffs and army boots.

"Deke wants to kill you," Ian said, laughing. "Hey, I gotta go, man. I'll catch you later, all right?"

"All right," Will said, and watched him walk back to the house.

"So, I guess this is it," he said to Amity.

She came and stood beside him on the sidewalk. "Yeah, I guess so."

"I hope you have a merry Christmas."

"Don't even call it that," she said. "It's like a million degrees here." She lifted a foot and extracted a pebble from her sandal, then flicked it onto the lawn. "I'm bummed we won't be able to give those people their presents. I was just thinking about that."

"It would have been fun," he said.

"I could tell you what I was going to get them," she said. "You could still buy the stuff."

"Nah. It'd be different, just one guy doing it."

"I guess so," she said.

"Of course, you could always come back," he said, and smiled, his heart pounding in his chest. "We could both get in the car right now."

She smiled with her eyes. "That's a fucked-up idea."

"You could do it, though."

She turned and glanced at the house. "I had a nice time, but I'm not going back. I can't."

"You're sure?"

"Yeah, I'm sure," she said, and something in her face seemed to close, so he believed her.

"Well, maybe I'll see you around sometime," he said.

"Maybe." She gave him the old expressionless stare, then turned and crossed the yard, her sandals snapping at her heels. As she opened the door, laughter rose in the living room. Will caught a glimpse of himself in the big window — a thin man standing in front of a car. He got in, started the engine, and pulled away from the curb. He was looking forward to the hospital now, more than he'd expected. Erroll, with his unending resources of optimism, seemed the man to spend time with.

Driving west on Tonelea Boulevard, he passed a few car lots and fast-food restaurants; then the suburbs gave way to red-earthed desert and cacti. Everything suddenly looked so odd it was hard to believe it had looked normal at one time, and that made him feel better. It was almost possible to imagine a time when the last several days might seem strange and far away, too, when he might look back on them with a kind of detached wonder. But he didn't want to let them pass too quickly. There was a pleasure to what he felt, along with the pain, and he understood that to let it go would be to suggest the worst of life — that it was transitory and random, quick to forget.

September

They lowered my lithium to four hundred milligrams and I can't tell any difference. I'm running in the mornings, which helps more than anything, I think. I get up at five and run hard for an hour, then spend the rest of the day in the air-conditioned library, trying not to get too intense about my schoolwork. I keep telling myself, You're in control, Tommy. You're in control. I work two shifts at La Casa Vieja, which is enough to pay for my classes. I still cut Mrs. Kmetko's lawn. Sometimes I'll drive by your old house on the way to school and see the lawn patchy and brown, the pyracantha turned the color of rust. Korean people live there now, they never water anything.

I went up to the house the other day, just hoping to see inside. A woman came out in a quilted silk housecoat, and I told her I was a housepainter. I don't think she understood. I saw the room, though — a deep red rug and the sun shining through the rear window. I could almost picture you reaching up to open the blinds, the light rolling over your body like a wave.

Everyone's away at school now — Rodney Olin, Carver Watts, all those guys from the team. I saw Alan Tuttle in the grocery store the day before he went back to U of A. He was in line with his mom, they had a bottle of champagne in their basket. I think they were embarrassed that I'd seen. She kind of laughed and said, "We're celebrating before he goes back. How are you, Tommy?"

"I'm all right."

I thought of all the times I'd gone to postgame parties at their house, and now Alan could hardly look me in the face.

Then I thought of the day you and I drank champagne at the Botanical Gardens, and it made me feel better. Sitting in the shade of those ironwood trees, talking to the old couple from Peru. It was the first time I'd had champagne, I didn't tell you at the time. I was shy, even though you knew my whole life story.

My dad is always on the couch when I get home, the TV on, a Shasta Grape or Lemon Lime on the table beside him. He wears his old navy-blue coveralls, though he hasn't worked in six months. Disability insurance pays for the rent and groceries. His emphysema hasn't gotten better, though he gave up smoking a year ago.

I'll come in and say, "Hey, Dad," and he'll say, "What's shakin', kid?" or something like that, but that's about as far as we get. He's not drinking now either, which I'm proud of him for, though it makes it harder to have a conversation. I've tried to tell him some of the things you thought I should say. One night, after we watched a Diamondbacks game, I just said, "Hey, Dad, all those problems I had, they weren't your fault. You know that, right?"

His eyes went wide like he was afraid of what I'd say next, but he nodded and said, "I know that, kid. Thanks for telling me, though."

"I'm going to be all right," I said.

He glanced at the TV. He's gotten so thin since he quit drinking you can see the bones beneath his skin.

I didn't get to the part about my brother. I don't think I ever will. I know Dad feels bad about Victor's death, and he probably blames himself for it. But he should know that it had more to do with Jess and the marines than anything *he* ever did. I don't like him feeling guilty when he's as sick as he is. I always knew, even when he was at his worst, that I'd end up feeling sorry for him.

I got a letter from Jason, he says he's doing all right. Of course, you know that. You probably hear from him every week. He says Berkeley's too big and the classes are hard, but I'm sure he's just making it sound bad so I'll feel better about going to junior college. He says Darren Barber flunked out of UCLA, which didn't surprise me. He got stoned all last semester, and now he's back working for his dad at a construction site in Chandler. I keep thinking he'll call, but I hope he doesn't. I don't want to hear from any of those guys.

I think about the first time I saw you, the day after Easter, when Jason brought me home to look at his collection of World War II planes. I barely knew him then. I'd just started talking to him in Arizona History, a skinny kid who no one else seemed to talk to. It was a few weeks after I got out of the hospital, I needed all new friends. My old ones didn't know what to say to me any more. It was exciting in a way, not having to worry about what people thought of me. I could talk to a guy like Jason, who was awkward and weird and smarter than anyone I'd ever known before.

We walked along the canal that day, the smell of carp and sage all around us, the sun cutting down through the power lines.

"So your dad's Mr. Deegan," I said, just trying to make conversation.

"Why? You ever had him?"

"Sophomore year."

He seemed suspicious, as if he thought I'd make fun of him. I could have said a lot about Mr. D., who'd been an asshole to me in Biology, but I wouldn't have done that. Instead we talked about Hopi civilization and World War II. As we approached your house, he gave me a worried look.

"My mom's deaf," he said. "She talks a little different."

I didn't know what to say to that. "So what?" is what I think I said.

We went inside, and I saw you in the kitchen, standing by the sink. You had Shannon on your hip, you'd just finished feeding her. There was a dark spot over your breast. It was the first thing I noticed about you.

When I mow Mrs. Kmetko's lawn the smell of gasoline makes my heart beat fast. I remember coming through your back door with grass in my socks, seeing you at the kitchen table, your hair filled with light, your heels tucked up against your thighs. Shannon would be in the back room, taking a nap, and we'd sit and drink iced tea and watch for the red lights on the baby monitor. If they didn't go on, it meant Shannon was asleep, and we'd end up in bed together. If they did, we'd pretend we'd never meant to do anything but drink iced tea and talk. You'd say, "Poor thing, I should check on her." And I'd go, "Yeah, I gotta get home anyway."

Those moments of waiting, of hoping. I remember how you'd smile at me when the monitor lights had been off for a while. It was like standing on a high cliff wall with the ocean below. It was like jumping.

(How we both knew it would happen that first time, I can't say. The way you looked at me, maybe. You told me you'd seen me play football, but it wasn't the way a mom would normally say it, more like a girl from school. I felt it in my chest. Even that first day we met, while Jason showed me his model airplanes, I was imagining what it would be like to kiss your throat, to put my hands on your waist. I'm not usually like that. It was your voice, I think, and the way your words tumbled into one another. Or the way you stared at my lips as I spoke. Through Jason's window, I noticed that the grass was high, and I knew I'd ask you about it. I knew I'd try to come back some Saturday when Jason and Mr. D. were busy with Scouts. I had it all planned before we'd said ten words to each other.)

The hardest part was sitting down with your family after we'd been together. I'd have mowed your lawn in the morning, then gone home smelling of sex and grass. In the shower, I'd have thought of all the things we'd done together, remembering every detail.

At dinner, Jason and Mr. D. would be talking about the school board or a senate hearing or the Heisenberg uncertainty principle. Mr. D.'s condescension was usually enough to relieve my guilt. He'd treat you like you were too stupid to follow the conversation, facing Jason as he spoke. Or he'd correct my grammar. I'd feel the secret between you and me, a line from your body to mine. Sometimes I'd catch your eye across the table and it was as good as having sex.

I drove by one of the houses I painted the summer before we met — one of the first ones, a Spanish-style house in the northeast part of Scottsdale. Sicilian umber on the outside, pearl inside, I think. I can hardly remember the houses. What I remember is smelling paint so high up my nose it was like smelling it with my brain, then going home and trying to sleep with my thoughts racing. I'd think about scaffolding and paint mixtures and my schedule for the coming week. Dr. Scanlon says I was trying to hide from my grief over Victor, and I'm sure he's right. I hardly thought about Victor at all in those days.

As soon as I bought that paint sprayer, things went through the roof. Now, of course, I know I should have cut back. But I liked the way people treated me, like a young entrepreneur. No one could tell I was manic, I don't know why. Maybe some people are like that normally. The Swedish couple from Camelback were so excited to get me, I'd painted the places on either side of them. They were like kids whose friends had gotten new bikes. Eight-fifty, I told them, twice what I'd told the others, but they snapped it up anyway. And then they came home and found me bleeding on the drop cloths in their dining room.

Victor would have been twenty-two on Friday. I went out to a place where we used to spend time together, Monkey Hills, a rolling field where we'd shoot BB guns and ride our bikes. Now there are surveyor's stakes in the ground everywhere, so they're probably turning it into a housing development.

I'd tag along with Victor and his friends, skinny kids with acne and bad personalities. Most of them didn't want me around. Sometimes Victor stuck up for me, sometimes not. They all liked the way I rode, though — full tilt, trying to prove myself. One time I laid down three rusted Safeway carts behind a ramp we'd built, then walked my bike to the top of King Monkey Hill. I got going as fast as I could, coming down, and hit the ramp and flew like Evel Knievel over the carts. I'm still not sure how I managed to land without killing myself.

"I bet he can't do that again," Steve Stoeffer said. He was just some weasel-faced friend of my brother's.

"Bet him," Victor said.

We put five dollars on the line, and I tried it again, but this time I clipped the last cart with my tire and flipped over the handle-bars. My body smacked the well-packed dirt. All the breath went out of me.

"He's all right," Victor said, running over. He untangled my legs and rolled me to my side so I could breathe. Then he turned to Steve and said, "Pay him."

"But he didn't do it," Steve said.

"You saw him do it the first time."

Sometimes I imagine you and Victor and I are downtown at the Phoenix Art Museum. I like to think you two would have gotten along. Victor wasn't into art as a kid, aside from drawing comic-book characters occasionally, but I think it's something he might have done if things had been different. He left a sketchbook at the house before he went back to the marines, and it was filled with drawings of the guys in his platoon. They were so good I could hardly believe he'd done them. I never even got the chance to tell him that.

Then there was what happened when I drove him to the bus station, when we saw that pyramid of river rocks off the side of the road. He got all excited about it, saying something about having a job like that, where you built things for the hell of it. I didn't encourage him. He'd been so weird, I just wanted him to be normal when he went back to the marines.

So I think of us going to the museum, looking at the Delacroix paintings and the sculptures by Rodin. Or you and I go to an apartment where he lives, one of those old brick buildings downtown. He's got a studio there and is inside working on a sculpture, bent over with an intense look on his face. He doesn't see us as we come in, then he turns around and grins.

The week Jason and your husband went to look at colleges was the best week of my life. I'd told my dad I'd be at Darren Barber's, working in the mornings at his dad's construction site, but I spent every night at your house. I'd kiss you before I went out to run in the morning, and I'd make sure the street was clear before I slipped back inside. I'd shower, and then we'd make love and lay with the covers bunched at our ankles, the sun throwing a square of light on the bed. When Shannon cried, you'd get up and feed her. I'd make breakfast. We'd spend the whole day together.

I enjoyed washing the dishes, making the bed, watching an HBO movie while Shannon played on the rug in front of us, just the ordinary things people do. After breakfast we'd work in the garden or you'd show me how to spin a clay bowl on the wheel. We each made one and fired them in the kiln, yours Indian red, mine aquamarine and lopsided.

I loved the way your consonants came out soft and aspirated. I loved your sudden, unselfconscious laugh. Sometimes you'd laugh so hard you had to sit on the floor with your head between your knees, and I'd see your face turn pink between your fingers. You taught me how to sign words like *grass* and *pancakes* and *Paris, France*. Sometimes you held a hand on my throat when I talked — so you could feel my voice, you said.

We talked about everything that had happened in our lives. I told you about my dad and Victor and the time I became a house-painting maniac. You told me about your wedding day: how you knew even then that you weren't in love with Mr. D. You were seventeen and pregnant, your father was a Pentecostal minister with strong ideas about everything. "What was I supposed to do?" you said, your voice so loud, as if you didn't know I was right beside you. I said you could do something *now*, told you a dozen times before you started to believe me, and then it was a thrill to see it register on your face — the possibility of a new life without Mr. D., taking Shannon to San Francisco or Boston or New York, enrolling in classes to finish your degree. We called Social Services and asked about disability grants, and suddenly it all seemed possible. And that's when it hit me: that when you left, you'd be leaving me, too. I don't know why I hadn't been thinking about that all along.

I remember waking up that last morning, seeing your face above me. You'd been telling me something while I slept. Your forehead was creased with worry, your eyes were red, but you smiled when you saw I'd woken.

"What were you saying?" I asked, but you never told me. You said, "I've got a plan for us today."

It was the day we went to the Botanical Gardens and drank champagne, the day we climbed the butte and saw a coyote standing on top of Hole in the Rock. Later we took Shannon to a toy store in Scottsdale, where I bought her a plush turtle. You bought me the silver ring I still wear. I'm wearing it now.

What are you doing now? I wonder. Have you gone to the places we talked about? Are you taking classes? I don't even have a place to picture you in, but I picture you anyway, in a little Dutch-white apartment with the San Francisco Bay out your window. You sit on a hardwood floor, reading from a textbook, my lopsided bowl beside you, filled with grapes. Shannon plays on a quilt by the window. Do you have a cat? I picture you with a cat, a short-haired black one. I like to think you're happy.

There's a counselor here who says I should transfer to Oberlin, his old school. He says they have good financial aid there. I got all A's in the spring, so it seems almost possible. Of course, even a mental defective could probably get A's at San Marcos. I'm amazed how much time I have now, not playing football.

I'm embarrassed about what I did in the Swedish couple's house, more so because things are going well for me now. It seems so melodramatic. Wherever Victor is now, he knows better than anyone that if I'd wanted to kill myself I would have just put a gun in my mouth and done it. I find it comforting to think that I *didn't* want to die. At the time it felt so much like I did.

I go out to Victor's grave in Tempe, near the old baseball park where we used to watch minor league games. Sometimes I feel like I'm close to him, like he must be all around, his spirit looking down the way people talk about. Other times I'm sure he's just another body in the ground, and it scares the hell out of me. I try to think about what I could have done to help him. It's something I'll think about the rest of my life. It's what made me do what I did in the Bjornsons' house, I'm sure. Dr. Scanlon tells me not to worry about it, says I couldn't have helped Victor anyway, but he's wrong about that. If Victor couldn't save himself, who *was* supposed to save him? My dad? The Marine Corps? What I'm learning these days is that I have to live with the fact that I *didn't* do all I could. Maybe we never do.

Lately I dream I'm playing football. It's that time of year, my body misses it, I guess. I dream I'm running a fade route, the wind singing through my face mask, the smell of grass in the air. I push past a cornerback and raise my arm, and the ball is there. I gather it in. Sometimes I'm taken down and the contact feels good, the crush of bodies against me. Other times I run alone into the end zone, but no one seems to know I have the ball. I look back and see the game going on without me.

There's a girl I see now, her name is Tara. You'd like her I bet. She's smart but she got bad grades in high school, like me, and now she's doing great here. We talk about our plans for the future, careful to keep them separate. She wants to go east, has friends at NYU. I feel older than she is most of the time, though she's actually a few months older than I am. We go to her mom's house after school and have sex on the little twin bed she's slept in since she was ten years old. It's strange; I feel like I'm being unfaithful to you sometimes, though that doesn't make any sense. On her walls are posters of the bands she used to like — Nine Inch Nails, Love and Rockets. She's got a nose ring and a tattoo of a devil on her ass. I always wanted a girlfriend like that, kind of punk, though she's not like that, really. And she's not really my girlfriend, either. She wouldn't call herself that.

There are things I know about myself that I wouldn't have known if it weren't for you. I know I can do well in school if I work hard enough, and I know that other people aren't as smart as I used to give them credit for.

I'm not sure how you understood these things about me, or if you were only trying to make me feel good by saying them, but it's made a difference in my life. I'm pretty sure I wouldn't be in school now if it weren't for you, and I know I wouldn't be thinking about Oberlin.

I wonder where you'd be if we hadn't done what we did together. Would you have left your husband? Would you have had the courage to do that? I like to think I had an effect on you, too.

―――――――――

In Jason's letter he talked about the time just before graduation, when we all went out for pizza at Emilio's. It was the night of the scholarship awards, Jason had received the Elks and the Arizona Republic grants. You were living in the apartment on Del Campo by that time, things were awkward between you and Mr. D. It was the night I called Mr. D. "Arthur," remember that? He looked at me with narrowed eyes, and I thought I'd given the whole thing away.

"Sorry, Mr. D.," I said, struggling to keep my voice from shaking. "It's the end of the year, I guess I'm just excited."

He huffed a laugh as if to say, What the fuck have *you* got to be excited about, Pendcrest? You didn't win any goddamn awards.

You caught my eye, thank God. Otherwise I might have told him everything.

After dinner, as Jason and I walked across the parking lot, he asked if I thought we'd still be friends when he went to Berkeley. I told him I didn't think so — or at least that's what he said in his letter. I don't remember saying it. What I remember is watching you put Shannon into the child seat of your Toyota, the neon lights of the restaurant flashing behind you. You got inside, turned the ignition, and drove out of the parking lot onto Yavapai Drive. I thought of you going to the little apartment on Del Campo, where we'd been together the night before. We wouldn't be together there tonight, because you were leaving for your sister's in a couple of weeks and we were trying to cool things off.

I didn't care whether Jason and I would be friends, not at the time. All I could think of was you.

―――――――――

I get brochures from schools all over the country now. Last month I just went crazy and sent out two dozen request forms. Stanford looks like a big Spanish village with a red-tiled bell tower. Princeton looks like a bunch of castle buildings and vines.

I wouldn't want to go to schools like those, the kids all look rich and smug, but I like to get the brochures. Maybe I'll drive out and see a few places this summer, if I can save the money. My counselor says I can think about any midlevel school that accepts transfers, and most of them do. I asked him if he thought the work would be hard for me, and he said I'd do all right. And I thought: *If I don't lose it again.* But these days I don't feel like I will.

I wonder what it would be like to see you again. I try not to think about it too much. The whole point of our being together was to prepare us for what would come next. I don't mind being alone now, and I don't mind working hard. There are times, though, when I miss you so badly I think I might crack. Do you get that way? Just times when I want to touch your skin and taste your breath and curl up against you. My life is going well and will get better, I hope, but I can't imagine it being as good as when Jason and your husband were looking at schools, when we had the house to ourselves and could do what we wanted. I wonder if there was a time when you felt that way too, when you thought, crazy as it seems, that we might end up together, that we might have a home and a life and a chance to live as a couple. Would you have wanted that, I wonder? Would you want it now? What were you saying that morning I woke up and saw you above me and your lips were moving?

1991
The Ant Generator,
Elizabeth Harris

Traps, Sondra Spatt Olsen

1990
A Hole in the Language,
Marly Swick

1989
Lent: The Slow Fast,
Starkey Flythe, Jr.

Line of Fall, Miles Wilson

1988
The Long White,
Sharon Dilworth

The Venus Tree,
Michael Pritchett

1987
Fruit of the Month,
Abby Frucht

Star Game, Lucia Nevai

1986
Eminent Domain,
Dan O'Brien

Resurrectionists,
Russell Working

1985
Dancing in the Movies,
Robert Boswell

1984
Old Wives' Tales,
Susan M. Dodd

1983
Heart Failure, Ivy Goodman

1982
Shiny Objects, Dianne Benedict

1981
The Phototropic Woman,
Annabel Thomas

1980
Impossible Appetites,
James Fetler

1979
Fly Away Home, Mary Hedin

1978
A Nest of Hooks, Lon Otto

1977
The Women in the Mirror,
Pat Carr

1976
The Black Velvet Girl,
C. E. Poverman

1975
*Harry Belten and the
Mendelssohn Violin Concerto,*
Barry Targan

1974
*After the First Death There Is No
Other,* Natalie L. M. Petesch

1973
The Itinerary of Beggars,
H. E. Francis

1972
The Burning and Other Stories,
Jack Cady

1971
*Old Morals, Small Continents,
Darker Times,*
Philip F. O'Connor

1970
The Beach Umbrella,
Cyrus Colter

Julie Orringer

A graduate of UC Berkeley and the Iowa Writers' Workshop, Ryan Harty grew up in Arizona and northern California. His stories have appeared in *Tin House*, the *Missouri Review*, and other magazines and have been anthologized in *The 2003 Pushcart Prize* and *The Best American Short Stories 2003*. He is a former Stegner Fellow at Stanford University and the recipient of a Henfield–Transatlantic Review Award. He currently lives in San Francisco with his wife, the writer Julie Orringer, and teaches at Stanford.